ROMANCING RAYNE

(SPECIAL FORCES: OPERATION ALPHA)

RILEY EDWARDS

This book is a work of fiction. Names, characters, places, and incidents are products of the author's imagination or used fictitiously. Any resemblance to actual events or locales or persons living or dead is entirely coincidental.

Dear Readers,

Welcome to the Special Forces: Operation Alpha Fan-Fiction world!

If you are new to this amazing world, in a nutshell the author wrote a story using one or more of my characters in it. Sometimes that character has a major role in the story, and other times they are only mentioned briefly. This is perfectly legal and allowable because they are going through Aces Press to publish the story.

This book is entirely the work of the author who wrote it. While I might have assisted with brainstorming and other ideas about which of my characters to use, I didn't have any part in the process or writing or editing the story.

I'm proud and excited that so many authors loved my characters enough that they wanted to write them into their own story. Thank you for supporting them, and me!

READ ON!

Xoxo

Susan Stoker

A SPECIAL THANK YOU

For Susan.

I cannot begin to express my gratitude for all your guidance and wisdom. You, my friend, are as kick-ass as they come. Your words not only inspire me but give me hours of enjoyment as I get lost in the worlds you create.

I hope you enjoy the recreation of Ghost and Rayne (with a Y and an E.).

xoxo

BEFORE YOU BEGIN

By now I think everyone knows what fan fiction is. But just in case you are unfamiliar, let me explain. Fan fiction is exactly what it sounds like. As a fan of the fabulous Susan Stoker I wrote Romancing Rayne solely based in her universe, using the characters, Ghost and Rayne from her book *Rescuing Rayne: Delta Force Heroes Book 1*. You will also see other characters from Susan's Delta Heroes series sprinkled throughout.

I have written this book as I, the reader, understood the characters. Though I am not Susan Stoker, I tried my hardest to stay true to the characters as she originally wrote them, but you will see differences. In keeping with my desire to render Rayne and Ghost as faithfully as possible, I read and reread *Rescuing Rayne* to give you the best book I could.

Romancing Rayne picks up after *Rescuing Mary*. While this book can be read as a standalone, I highly recommend you read Susan's Delta Force Heroes before reading *Romancing Rayne*. Not only will you get a better insight into Ghost and Rayne, but the series is phenomenal, and a must read! (And the first book is currently FREE!)

Grab your copy here

*I have used celebrities and noteworthy public figures in a fictitious fashion. I make no claim that the manner in which I used their likenesses is true in any way. The characters I based around their celebrity are fictional and done in the spirit of light-hearted fun.

I hope you enjoy *Romancing Rayne* as much as I enjoyed creating it for you.

Sign up for the **Riley's Rebels** mailing list to receive a **FREE COPY of Unbroken** and stay up to date on releases, sales, and giveaways.

https://www.subscribepage.com/rileyedwardsfreebook

1

Rayne

"You may kiss your bride."

At the officiant's declaration, the room erupted, the cheers and whooping a startling contrast to the solemn silence while we exchanged our vows.

Ghost didn't move, and his smile faded.

"Ghost, kiss me," I whispered.

"Not yet, Rayne." Pure love shone in his eyes. "I'll never forget this moment. How beautiful you look in your dress. Us promising our lives to each other. None of it. You've made me the happiest man in the world."

"Kiss me," I urged, needing to feel his lips on mine.

"With pleasure."

I vaguely heard Truck and Mary being presented as husband and wife for the second time. But between the magic of Ghost's kiss and the crowds' renewed cheers, I was lost in my husband.

Husband.

He pulled back, turned us toward our friends, and waited for Truck to finish devouring Mary. We did it. The silly marriage pact Mary and I had made all those years ago had finally come to fruition. Ghost's hand tightened around mine, and I knew he was just as happy for our friends as I was. Though, I wished Truck would hurry up; I had a surprise for Ghost, and it was burning a hole in my pocket.

By the time we made our way down the aisle toward the exit of the church, I was nearly jogging. Ghost, Truck, Beatle, and Blade had said they wanted the biggest celebration our town had ever seen, but I had no idea they'd meant something this large. The church had been standing room only, filled with scores of people I'd never met. I looked out over the sea of uniforms; Navy and Army seemed to fill most the room, however I'd bet I'd find police, fire, and some Texas Rangers among the crowd as well. It was a beautiful testament to how well respected the team was.

"In a hurry?" Ghost chuckled when I tugged on his hand after he'd stopped to say hello to Wolf and Caroline.

"My feet hurt," I lied.

With a nod, he lifted me in his arms and continued to the waiting limo.

"Put me down."

"Not a chance."

He placed me in the back seat and arranged my dress, making me thankful I hadn't worn one of those huge, puffy, frilly dresses some brides dream of, opting, instead, for something simple and elegant, *and* it had cool, hidden pockets—perfect for holding my surprise.

We pulled away from the curb, and suddenly I was nervous. I was being silly; I knew Ghost would be happy, but now I was questioning the timing.

"Have I told you how beautiful you look?" he started.

"A few times, yes. Ghost?"

"Yeah, Princess?"

"Thank you."

"I hope today was everything you dreamed it would be," he said.

I thought back and tried to remember a time I'd ever been this happy and found I couldn't. I was right where I was supposed to be, and not a moment too soon.

"How could it not be? I married the man of my dreams, my super-secret spy."

Ghost chuckled, and I continued, "Thank you for waiting, for being so patient. Thank you for loving me and wanting to share your life with me."

There had been days I'd felt horrible for making Ghost wait for us to get married. But after today, I knew in the marrow of my bones, everything happened for a reason.

"There's no place I'd rather be than by your side."

On a deep exhale, I turned to fully face him.

"Most of all, thank you for giving me this."

I reached into my pocket and pulled out the pregnancy test, showing him the results.

"Are you . . .? Are we . . .?" he stuttered. "You're having my baby, Rayne?"

I nodded, too overcome with emotion to verbally answer.

Ghost

I tried to keep my hand steady as I stared at the word PREGNANT displayed in the digital window. It was amazing how a simple piece of plastic could forever change your life. I thought my life had been complete a few minutes ago when Rayne became my wife. I'd never been more wrong. This baby only added to my already full heart.

Placing the proof I was going to be a father in the pocket of my suit jacket, I reached for the phone connected directly to the chauffeur.

"Drive around and don't stop until I tell you."

"Ghost! We can't be late. Everyone's waiting for us."

"Princess, they've been waiting years for you to

make an honest man out of me. Another hour won't kill them."

"An hour?"

"Oh, yeah. We have a lot to celebrate, and when I'm done with you, there'll be no doubt just how thankful I am."

Her protest died when I covered her perfect lips with mine.

I, indeed, spent the next hour making sure my wife knew she was more than worth the wait.

Wife.

2

Ghost

Rayne's discomfort was palpable. It had started this morning when we woke up and continued all the way to the airport. Now that we'd boarded the aircraft, she was practically vibrating with anxiety.

"Rayne? Rayne Jackson, is that you?" the flight attendant said from beside me.

Rayne's face lit up, and she stood.

"Lou Anne. Oh my God. It's been forever." After some careful maneuvering Rayne was in the aisle, pulling the older woman in for a hug. "I can't believe you're still on the international run."

"You know me. I love the adventure."

While her smile remained, the light had dimmed in Rayne's eyes. There was a time when my wife had been adventurous, too. The first day I met her she'd told me about her exploits, dinner at the Eiffel Tower, gondola rides in Italy, she'd even smoked a joint in Amsterdam. But that was before Egypt. Before she'd been caught in the middle of a plot to overthrow the government. Before I'd found her shackled to a bed. No. I couldn't go there. This trip was supposed to be about making new memories, not dwelling on the past.

Lou Anne must have noticed the change in Rayne and changed topics.

"So, London? First stop or will you be staying?"

"Staying. It's our honeymoon." Rayne lifted her left hand and showed off her ring. "Rayne Bryson—as of yesterday."

My heart swelled hearing Rayne say her new name.

Lou Anne looked down at me and smiled. "Girllll . . ." She drew out the L and Rayne laughed.

"I know, right? Meet my husband Keane." I stood and offered her my hand. "Lou Anne and I used to work international runs together."

"Nice to meet you."

"The pleasure is all mine. I always knew Rayne would catch herself a hunk. Do you have any brothers?" She added a wink, and I instantly liked Lou Anne. She had spunk for a woman who looked like she was nearing seventy.

"Afraid not."

I caught Rayne around the middle and pulled her

out of the aisle before a man with a suitcase far too large for the overhead compartments could jostle her.

"A gentleman, too. I'll be around later, duty calls." She gestured toward the man with the offending luggage and followed after him.

"A hunk, huh?"

Rayne rolled her eyes and settled back into her seat. "Of course, you wouldn't miss that."

An hour into our flight, Rayne's eyes kept shifting around the cabin. I wasn't sure if it was an occupational hazard or nerves. But it was something akin to torture seeing her so uncomfortable. Grateful first-class seating only allowed two to a row and a fold up armrest, I tugged Rayne over and wrapped my arm around her.

"Relax."

"I'm trying. I don't want to ruin this trip."

"There's nothing you could do to ruin anything."

She cuddled into my side and slowed her breathing.

"Remember the first time we were in London together?"

"How could I forget?" Her arm tightened across me. "Best decision I ever made sitting down next to a handsome stranger."

"No, the best decision was checking my ID and sending it to Mary before you'd let me take you to lunch."

"Nope. That may've been my smartest one. But the best certainly was seeing you across the room and deciding to chat you up."

"Chat me up?" I laughed.

"Well, yeah. I did most of the talking. You sat there staring at me, trying to figure out why a crazy person was talking to you."

"No, Princess. I was devising a plan to get a sexy woman to go to the hotel with me."

"Dog." She gently slapped my chest. "Doubtful. I was in my airline uniform, nothing sexy about that."

"No, but imagining what was underneath was driving me wild. And when we were in the taxi on the way to the city, I was trying as discretely as possible to adjust my cock in my pants. It was a long ride, and I was pretty sure I was going to have permanent marks from my zipper."

"Well, it's a good thing there were no lasting side effects."

"It was touch and go there for a while. Especially after you kissed me. You tasted like heaven. I had never been so hard in my life from a single kiss. It was killing me. I think that's when I started falling in love with you."

Rayne

I knew what Ghost was doing, and while I appreciated him, reminding me of the first time we kissed had me squirming in my seat.

"You've never told me that."

"It's the truth." He kissed the top of my head, and I wished we were alone so he could kiss other places.

"Hmm. I don't know if I like that all it took was me giving you a hard-on for you to fall in love," I teased.

"It wasn't the hard-on."

"No?"

"No. It was the promise behind the kiss."

"The promise?"

"The promise of a beautiful life. Something I never thought I'd have. The promise of you." Ghost's hand came up and covered mine where it rested on his chest before he brought our combined hands lower until he finally stopped over his crotch and held them there. "And every day since then, all I have to do is think about you and this happens."

"Even on a mission?"

"Yes. Even then."

"That sounds uncomfortable."

"It is." I couldn't contain my laughter at the images he was provoking. "What's funny?"

"All I can picture is you chasing a terrorist with a tent pole in your pants, leaving them to wonder if you're hiding another pistol in there."

"A pistol? Try a .50 cal BMG." Ghost lifted his hips

and pushed his hard-on into my palm, reminding me exactly what he had hiding under his cargo pants.

Ghost tightened his arm around me, making me feel safe and protected, just like he'd done the day he'd rescued me in Egypt and every day since.

My nervousness turned to excitement, and I couldn't wait until we landed.

3

Ghost

Turbulence jostled me awake, giving me the perfect opportunity to watch Rayne sleep. I thought back to the pregnancy test she'd given me in the limo and my pulse began to race. We'd debated whether or not to tell our friends and after some consideration, we'd decided to keep it to ourselves until we got back.

Mary knew, Rayne had confessed to telling her first and, in a way, I was happy she had. Their friendship had suffered some blows in the past few months. Even though Mary and Rayne had repaired what had been broken, they needed this. A secret between them. Something just the two of them knew. Besides, I was sure there was some woman code that said the best friend must know all the important stuff before the husband.

It sounded counterproductive considering a secret was what had torn our group apart in the first place. If I've learned anything since being with Rayne, it was that women thought differently than men. There was no use trying to figure out why they did and said what they did. After Emily, Harley, Kassie, Casey, Wendy, and even Bryn and Sadie came into our lives it was confirmed that women will stick together and gang up on the men whenever they could. And not a single man on my team would have it any other way. We go into battle together; we fight, kill, and are willing to die for one another. But the women? They're just as much a team as we are. They rally around each other when we're gone and none of them would allow any of the others to be alone. They've forged deep bonds and had the same commitment to their girl pack as the guys had to the team. No woman was ever left behind. I loved that Rayne had that. It made going on missions a little easier knowing her girls would take care of her while I was gone. And our baby would have that, too.

Annie was going to flip. The little spitfire had barreled into our lives with a determination I'd never witnessed before. There was never a question she was Fletch's child and that meant she was ours, too. Between her new brother and honorary cousins, I had a feeling she'd be roping them into a whole lot of trouble and I couldn't wait.

"Ghost?" Rayne's sleep-rough voice pulled me from my thoughts.

"Yeah, Princess?"

"Are we almost there?"

"About another hour," I told her after consulting my watch.

She rubbed her eyes and sat up, looking around the plane, and I could see the trepidation was back.

In the dark recesses of my mind, I was happy she'd have to quit her job at the airline after the baby was born. Hell, I'd be fucking thrilled if she quit now. Not that I'd ever tell her that. I wanted her to do whatever made her happy, but I'd be lying if I said her flying around to different cities didn't make me uneasy. Especially while I was out of the country. If that made me an asshole, I didn't care. I needed to know she was safe at home, around her tribe, while I was gone.

"Let's play a game," I suggested.

Rayne put the bottle of water she'd been drinking back in her purse and smiled.

"A game?"

"Word association."

Recognition dawned, and she laughed.

"Are you trying to get me into bed?"

"It worked well the first time."

"Ghost!"

"What? You looked like you were ready to jump out

of bed and bolt. I needed to think of something to keep you there."

That wasn't necessarily the truth. She had looked nervous, but I wanted to get to know her. At the time, it was selfish of me. I should've kept my distance, especially knowing I was leaving in the morning. But somewhere deep in my bones, I knew she was the one. I knew she belonged to me, only I wasn't ready. As hard as it was, I'd stupidly thought I had to let her go.

"Fine. Let's play your game," she huffed.

I tried to think of a word to start with, but I was too distracted by the way Rayne was fidgeting in her seat. There was heat behind her stare, and I knew that look.

"Dream?"

Her cheeks blushed, and I knew I was on the right track. What in the hell had the little minx been dreaming of?

Rayne

I should've known nothing would slip by Ghost. I was having the most erotic dream when the plane dipped and shook me awake. Now I couldn't get the images out of my mind.

"Mile high club."

"Come again?" The shock on his face was priceless.

Being a flight attendant for as long as I'd been, I'd

seen it all. Couples trying to discretely slip into the lavatory together or trying to conceal their very obvious movements under a thin airline provided blanket. Let's just say those blankets were tossed rather than going back into circulation. Gross! I myself had never considered it, the thought of trying to get it on in a small, cramped space never sounded appealing, or sexy. However, the images my dream had provoked had me squeezing my legs together trying to get some relief.

"You heard me."

"You horny, baby?" he whispered in his best Austin Powers impersonation, which sucked.

"Not anymore after that lame attempt at a joke."

He pulled the blanket fully over my lap, and his hand stilled on my thigh.

"Not anymore, huh?"

"I thought we were playing a game," I reminded him.

"We are. It's your turn."

I glanced out the small window, nothing but dark, puffy clouds as far as the eye could see.

"Storm?"

"Heathrow," he replied then asked, "London?"

"My first one-night stand." I laughed when his smile faded.

"Really?" he mocked. "I'm seeing a theme here."

"What's the . . ." The rest of my question died in my

throat as Ghost's hand traveled higher, stopping just shy of where I needed it to be.

His fingers continued to rub over my jeans when he leaned in closer and whispered, "My beautiful wife needs to be taken care of." The rumble of his voice sent goose bumps racing down my arms.

He wasn't wrong, but we still had an hour before we landed and another hour after that before we'd be alone.

"Come on." His hand left my leg, and he grabbed mine, giving me a firm tug.

"Where are you going?" I whispered, trying not to wake the sleeping passengers around us.

"Not, me. Us." He stepped into the aisle and continued to pull me behind him.

"No way."

Ghost didn't stop until he made his way to the first-class galley where, much to my embarrassment, Lou Anne was restocking the coffee on her cart.

"Hey, guys. If you needed something, you could've hit the call button." She beamed. Ghost glanced at the green, unoccupied sign on the bathroom door and it was a race between me and Lou Anne whose blush appeared faster. I imagined mine did, considering my cheeks felt like they were on fire.

"Oh! Ohhhh!" Her eyes widened, and she smiled. "Sorry. I'll just switch this to out of order for you." She reached into a cabinet and retrieved the rectangular plaque and placed the magnetic, *inoperative,* sign on the door and wagged her perfectly manicured eyebrows at Ghost. What the hell was going on? It was against airline policy to close a fully operational lavatory, and there had to be some FAA rule against sex in an aircraft that I should've known. However, at that moment I was so shocked I couldn't think of it.

Ghost winked, yes, he winked, at Lou Anne and started to pull me toward the tiny bathroom. He was in for a rude awakening if he thought we'd both fit in the small space. The stall was larger in first class than in the world traveler, economy section but it was still an airplane lavatory.

"Huh?" He looked around trying to puzzle out how we were both going to fit.

I couldn't stop the laugh that bubbled up.

"You think this is funny?" he asked.

"So funny. Didn't think this through, did you, super-spy?"

"Oh, Princess, I'll have your jeans around your ankles and you up against the door in two seconds. We'll see who's laughing then."

My laughter died, and suddenly my mouth was dry.

He was serious.

"It's not possible," I argued.

"Anything's possible. I've been in tighter situations than this."

"Really?"

"Really."

Obviously tired of our conversation in front of the restroom he tugged my hand, moving us until he could close the door. With my back against the cool metal and his broad, muscular chest pressed to my front he leaned down to whisper, "Now I have you just where I want you."

Oh, shit. This was happening.

4

Ghost

The space may have been designed for a single person, but there was no way that was going to deter me. Between Rayne admitting she'd had some sort of dirty dream and the ever-present need I had whenever I was near her, it was too tempting. Not to mention, the thought of joining the mile-high club and giving her another first was too thrilling to pass up. Yes, I'd make it work.

"So, tell me, what were you dreaming about?" I kissed the side of her neck, and when her head fell to the side, giving me better access, I moved lower to the front of her throat, right where I knew she loved. Rayne didn't disappoint when she moaned as I sucked on the sensitive area.

"You were kissing me."

"Was I kissing you here?" I moved the collar of the V-neck shirt she was wearing to the side and placed a few small, open-mouthed kisses on her shoulder.

"No."

"Here?" I yanked her shirt up, exposing her perfect tits and took a moment to admire the swell of cleavage. So fucking beautiful. I had to taste the milky-white flesh overflowing the confines of her bra. I wished I had more time. I wanted to spend hours sucking and licking her perfect nipples hidden behind the lacey material. Later. There would be plenty of time for that tonight, and every night for the rest of our lives.

"No."

"Then where, Princess?"

"Lower."

The groan that slipped from my mouth sounded more like a growl, and Rayne shivered in my arms. Yeah, she liked that, too, when my voice deepened, and my touch became demanding. That was when my wife lost control.

"Tell me exactly where."

"My . . ." She trailed off, and I nipped her puckered nipple through her bra. "My clit."

I had to take a few calming breaths to get myself under control.

"As much as I'd love to tongue your clit until you're thrashing around and screaming your orgasm, that will have to wait until tonight. For now, we're going to have to make do with my cock." I quickly unbuttoned her jeans, pushed them down to her knees, and went to work removing one sneaker before I maneuvered her out of one pant leg. Happy with my progress I looked up, coming face-to-face with her closely trimmed curls. I buried my face in her pussy the best I could and licked every inch I could reach. Frustrated with the lack of space and the time restraint I knew we were under, I stood and took her mouth in a kiss, making sure there was no doubt how much I wanted her. Fuck, my wife could kiss. Her tongue dueled and danced with mine while still allowing me to set the pace. She was perfect.

Rayne went about unfastening my pants at the same time my hand went to her now uncovered pussy. I slipped a finger inside, and my cock twitched at the tight, wet heat that welcomed me. As soon as she had my cock free, I pulled her leg up around my hip and in a single thrust, I was balls deep.

"Ghost!"

"Sh. Quiet. This is going to have to be quick, Princess."

I kept my thrusts fast and forceful, not having time to work her up the way I normally would. Needing a better angle, I pressed her harder against the door and moved my hands to her ass. With a quick lift, both her legs were around my waist and her arms went around my neck. The new position allowed me to go deeper, and the tightness of her heat threatened to unman me.

"Jesus, you feel so fucking good," I whispered. "Take one of your hands and rub your clit for me. I need you ready."

Rayne did as I asked and moaned. Damn sexy, but too fucking loud. I brought my lips to hers and spoke quietly. "I can't wait until we get to the hotel and I can put you on your knees and see the tattoo I love so much on your back as I take you from behind." Her pussy spasmed, and I had to close my eyes to keep my orgasm at bay. "Princess, get there." Before she could respond, our lips met and once again I was lost in her —consumed. Her body shook in my arms and she wrenched her mouth from mine.

"Ghost!"

"Come with me, Rayne."

5

Rayne

"Remember the first time we were in a taxi together?" I asked after Ghost and the driver situated our luggage in the trunk, or the boot as they called it in England, and Ghost climbed in beside me.

"Every minute," he replied.

"That's doubtful since it wasn't all that exciting."

The taxi maneuvered around the busy airport traffic, and I was curious if he knew where he was going.

"Did you tell the driver where to take us?"

"I did. Now stop fishing for clues and sit back and enjoy the ride."

Damn. I was hoping now that we'd arrived, Ghost would finally tell me about the plans he'd made. The suspense was driving me crazy.

"You know I don't like surprises," I tried again to get him to spill the beans.

"Yes, you do. You'll know soon enough." He pulled me closer to him and kissed the top of my head. "Tell me what you remember about our first taxi ride together."

"I remember thinking the T-shirt you were wearing was a little dirty."

I thought back and couldn't help but smile; from the moment I'd clapped eyes on him in the airport I was so drawn to him I'd done something out of character and approached him. He was sitting alone, his back to the wall, eyes assessing everything. It was as if there was a magnetic pull, and with each step I took it got stronger.

"My shirt was dirty?" He chuckled.

"Also, you looked a little scruffy, but even in your disheveled state I could still see your muscles flexing and I wanted to touch them—without the wrinkled, days-worn shirt covering them."

"Is that all?"

"No. I wanted to know you more than I wanted to see you naked. There was something about you that made butterflies swarm in my stomach, something exciting and scary at the same time. And even though all I knew about you was your name was John Benbrook from Fort Worth, Texas, I knew you'd change my life."

"I'm—"

"Don't apologize. It's part of our story, and I wouldn't change a thing." As the silence continued, I mentally berated myself for bringing up the fact I hadn't known his real name the first time we were together. Sure, when I found out he'd lied it'd stung but I quickly came to understand why he'd used an alias. "I'm serious; it's part of our journey—part of why I fell in love with you."

"How's that?" He still didn't look convinced, and I searched for the words to make him understand.

"First, I'd like to point out that while your ID said your name was John, you never hid your identity from me. You told me to call you Ghost, and that's who you are, the real you. It's funny to think about, but how many times have I called you Keane? Hell, most of the time I forget that's your name."

His lips twitched, and I was happy to see his smile starting to return. "The man I fell in love with, the man you are, has a reason to conceal his name from the world. You save people, you put your life in jeopardy every time you go on a mission. You're my real-life superhero. So, whether you introduced yourself as John, Jack, Leon, or Keane, it never mattered. I always knew the man behind the name."

"Thank you, Princess."

"So, what were you thinking once you successfully got me into the taxi?"

He was quiet for a moment, and I hoped he wasn't still stuck on the name thing. It had been years ago, water under the bridge. We'd worked past all those feelings, especially after he'd come home from the first mission he'd gone on after we were together. Mary had driven down to Killian with me, and when Ghost gave me shit about being there, Mary, being Mary, meaning she always had my back, went on the warpath. It was a wake-up call about just how dangerous his job really was.

Without thought my hand went to his arm, and I rubbed the faint scars left from the skin graft he'd received. We got lucky that deployment. If the explosion had been any closer, none of the guys would've made it back alive. After that, any minor obstacle in our way, like a first name, seemed trivial.

Ghost

I hadn't thought about John Benbrook in a long time. I had those fake credentials in my safe and still had to use them from time to time. Hell, each of us on the team had a drawer full of bogus passports, driver's licenses, press passes, and TWIC cards. You name it, we had it in a variety of names. It was a long time ago and something that was necessary, but I still hated that was how we'd met. The first time I made love to Rayne, she thought I was John. I never thought she'd forgive me; fuck, I hadn't known how to forgive myself until Beatle reminded me I'd told her my call sign. That was who I really was. But I'd still been untruthful, and the one thing I wasn't was a liar.

"Ghost?" Rayne's voice snapped me back to the present.

"What do you remember about our first taxi ride together?" she repeated.

"For the first time in my life, I hated my job. I had this beautiful, sexy, intelligent, funny, spunky woman sitting next to me and I couldn't keep her. And I wanted to. I remember sitting next to you and for a brief moment I could see what my life would be with you by my side. Then reality set in and I hated I had to let you go."

We both fell silent, and I was surprised I'd admitted that to Rayne. I loved being a Delta. I loved my team. But in that moment, I'd wished I'd been anything but a highly trained, special forces operator.

"I couldn't imagine you being anything else," she said and quickly covered her mouth, stifling a yarn. "Sorry, I'm so tired all the time now."

"You need to rest. I'll wake you when we get there." She moved her hand off my arm and settled in, one hand resting on her belly, the other secure in my grasp.

Thank God, fate had brought her back to me.

GHOST

“Princess, we’re here.”

Her eyes slowly came open, but when she saw where we were she shot up to an upright position. Now fully awake, she took in her surroundings.

“Seriously?” she gasped.

The look of surprise was worth the weeks of pestering, begging me to tell her the plans I’d made for our honeymoon.

The Park Plaza was a gamble. It was the hotel we’d stayed at the night we’d met but also the place I’d left her in the early morning hours. I’d snuck out of the bed we’d shared and left nothing more than a “thank you for last night” note with the front desk. I shook the thought from my head and focused on the present and the happiness that shone in Rayne’s eyes.

“Come on, let’s get inside.”

By the time we made it to the curb, the driver had our bags waiting; a quick thank you and exchange of money and we were on our way. We only had a few days in London, and I was excited to start our honeymoon.

I was happy to see everything seemed to be the same, modern with a mix of old world opulence. It was classy, yet still inviting and exactly what I’d been hoping for. A perfect recreation of our first trip but with the fairytale ending Rayne deserved.

"The lobby is just like I remember it, but this time it feels different." Rayne laughed.

"How so?"

"Well, the first time you checked us into this hotel, I felt like I had "one-night stand" tattooed on my forehead. This time, I feel like Mrs. Rayne Bryson, the proud wife of Ghost Bryson."

"Come on, crazy woman, we have lots to do. Are you hungry?"

"Starving. I think by the time this baby comes, I'm going to be as big as a house."

"A beautiful house."

"Ghost!" she admonished.

"What? I'm just agreeing with you." Before I could insert my foot any further into my mouth, the woman checking us in interrupted, needing my attention.

With room keys in hand, we headed for the elevators.

"I hope we have a good view," Rayne said as she peered through the glass enclosure overlooking the main lobby of the hotel.

I didn't answer, not wanting to spoil her surprise. When the elevator stopped on our floor, she was too busy digging through her handbag to notice her surroundings. I led her to the room, unlocked the door, and pushed it open, allowing her to enter before me.

"I can't believe I can't find my Chapstick," she complained, still looking through her purse. "I hate how dry my lips get when I . . . holy shit . . . Ghost!" Her gaze had finally lifted, and she was looking around the room. Lip balm forgotten, she tossed her bag on the bed and went straight for the window.

"I can't believe you did this." She turned to face me, tears streaming down her pretty cheeks. "Our room. You brought us back to our room." She continued to cry, and I prayed they were happy tears.

Leaving the luggage by the door, I moved to where Rayne was standing and pulled her into my arms.

"Princess?"

"I knew it."

"Knew what?"

"Remember when we were at Westminster Abbey?" Rayne turned in my arms to face the window.

"Of course."

"You told me you weren't romantic, and I remember explaining to you all the ways you were. From how you'd paid for everything we'd done, to always holding the door open, allowing me to enter first. You were protective and never allowed anyone to bump into me or get too close. You let me see everything I wanted to see without complaint. I knew you didn't believe me and only agreed to make me be quiet. But, Ghost, you are the most romantic man I've ever known. You show me a hundred times a day how much you love me, you still protect me, you always make sure I have the best seat when we're out. You always clean the house before I get back from a trip so I don't have to do a single thing but relax. You take care of me, and us, and our home. So, I've always known you were a closet romantic, but I also knew you wanted to believe in the fairytale."

"Princess," I started.

"Don't argue. I knew it then and know it more than ever now."

She was mostly right, but she was also wrong.

"You still don't get it. It's you, Princess, only you. I want you to have everything you ever dreamed of having. The romance, the flowers, the happily ever after fairytale. I'll move heaven and earth to make sure you have everything you need and to make sure you're safe and protected."

"I know you will." Rayne turned to face me, rolling up on her tiptoes she kissed the corner of my mouth. "You've proven it daily. Now come on and feed me and the baby."

The baby.

Before she could step away, I brought her wrist to my lips and kissed the tiny scars left from her time in Egypt. Scars that reminded me fate had brought us together not once, but twice.

6

Rayne

"It even smells the same," I noted when we made our way into Mickey's. I looked around the small restaurant and nothing had changed; even the menu on the chalkboard behind the long counter was the same.

"Fish," Ghost deadpanned.

"Well, yes, and potatoes and grease."

"It's a good thing you're not in advertising. I'm not sure your description of fish, grease, and potatoes whets the appetite." Ghost laughed and pushed us forward to the counter where a young woman was waiting to take our order. "Two fish and chips, please."

Without letting go of my hand Ghost navigated the busy pub, stopping at a table in the corner. He pulled my chair out, as always, before taking his seat across from me, with his back to the wall.

"We should've carved our names into the table," I told him, running my hand over the worn, chipped wood.

"Hold that thought," he said and got up, then disappeared into the crowd, returning a few moments later with the most delicious smelling baskets of yummy fried fish and French fries. I wasn't sure what Ghost's issue was with my description of the place was; the fried batter from the fish and greasy crispy fries looked and smelled divine.

I didn't wait for Ghost to sit back down before I picked up a thick-cut fry and popped it in my mouth. So good. Just as I remembered.

"You know what's funny?" Ghost asked. I shook my head, unable to answer with another piece of delicious, greasy goodness in my mouth. "Back home, you only order fries if they're the thin, crispy ones. You won't even eat the ones at the bar on base because you say they're too thick. But you devour them here."

"Hmm? You're right." My hand stopped short of my mouth as I pondered his statement. Not so much about how I preferred my food but that he'd noticed. Ghost paid attention to everything, part of that was because he was a Delta, and they were aware of their surroundings at all times, even when home. However, the fact he remembered and cared enough to make changes to fit my preferences was something *I'd* never paid attention to. Thinking about it made my heart swell. After I'd made the comment about the fries at the bar not being to my liking, we'd never gone back there. Whenever I said I wanted a burger, even though Ghost loved to go and have a beer and play darts after our meal, we went to a burger joint downtown. He was always doing things like that for me. Small, simple stuff that individually didn't seem like a big deal. But all of it mattered. All of it put together was one more way he showed he loved me and would always put me first.

"I love you, Ghost."

"I love *you*, Princess. So, I was thinking. I like your idea about carving our names in the table."

"We can't do that."

"Not our names, but our initials."

"Ghost," I scolded. "That's like destruction of property or something. We can't really do it. It's against the law."

"Only if we get caught."

Was he crazy? Carving your initials was something teenagers did. What was next? Was he going to put a heart around our names, too?

"That way, next time we're here, we can retrace our steps and find all the places we marked," he continued.

"Next time?"

"Yep. Mrs. Rayne Bryson, I promise to bring you

back to London for a proper scavenger hunt on our twenty-fifth anniversary."

And he still wanted to deny he wasn't a romantic.

"Okay."

"That trip, we'll mark more places so on our fiftieth anniversary we'll have more to find."

"Fiftieth? Ghost, we'll be too old in fifty years to walk the streets of London."

"I'll never be too old to take care of you. Twenty-five, fifty, one hundred years from now, I'll always make sure you have everything your heart desires."

There it was again, Ghost doing what Ghost did best, making me feel loved and protected and, above all, he made me feel cherished.

"For our fiftieth anniversary, we'll rent those power scooters and zoom around the streets making everyone get out of our way."

"Do I look like a man who would be caught riding a power scooter, or a motorized wheelchair?"

"No." I laughed at the thought of Ghost in a wheelchair; that was never going to happen. Though I could imagine him with salt and pepper hair and still as hot as ever.

We finished our meals and piled the empty baskets and napkins in the middle of the table, then Ghost reached into his pocket, pulling out a small knife.

"I'll do the honors, so you don't cut yourself. You tell me where."

I looked around the room full of people; no one was necessarily paying attention, but we were still out in the open.

"Do you need me to stand watch or something?" I whispered.

Ghost threw his head back and roared with laughter. I wasn't sure what was funny but seeing him carefree and happy was one of the best feelings in the world.

"No, Princess. This isn't a top-secret, covert mission. Just point where you want it."

"Don't laugh at me. I don't want you to get arrested, leaving me to wander around London by myself for the next few days."

"Never gonna happen." He quickly sobered. "I would never do anything that would jeopardize your safety or mine."

He didn't wait for me to show him where I wanted our initials, instead, he chose the corner closest to him and left a very tiny P+G.

Princess and Ghost.

Ghost

By the time we exited the Waterloo station the sun had started to set. There was one more place I wanted to take Rayne before we headed back to the hotel.

"How are you feeling?"

"Wonderful." She beamed, her smile so full of love it nearly took my breath away.

"You're not too tired? I don't want you to overdo it. We have a long day tomorrow, but I want to make one more stop before we call it a night."

"But it's still early," she protested.

"It is."

I tucked Rayne close as we walked toward the River Thames.

"I'm not tired, and it's only like four in the afternoon back home."

"I'm sure I can find plenty of ways to exhaust my pretty wife." She tucked her head against my chest and wrapped her arms around me.

"In that case, I'm ready to go back now."

"Come on. I wanna show you something. Then I'm taking you back to the hotel to feast on your sweet pussy. The little taste on the plane did nothing to satisfy my hunger."

"Do I get to taste you, too?" she shyly asked, her words muffled.

"Oh, yeah. You can have anything you want."

The rest of the short walk to the Eye of London was done in silence, both of us content, holding each other and taking in the sights. When we stopped in front of the gigantic Ferris wheel, she pulled away and looked up.

"It seems bigger than before."

I bit back the juvenile, "that's what she said," response and opted instead to pull her to the Fast Track and Private Capsule entry area.

"What, no bribing the attendant this time?" She nodded at the sign.

"Best fifty pounds I ever spent. Having you all alone, watching you take in the night sky was worth every penny."

"I'm still not so sure about this."

"Come on, you're safe with me."

A sense of déjà vu came over me, transporting me back years before when we stood at that very spot, waiting for the capsule to stop and allow us entry. I had only known Rayne a few hours, yet I knew with great clarity she'd forever altered my life. I'd spoken those exact words to her, both in coaxing her onto the ride and once again when we were at the top. She'd called me John then, the name making my gut clench in distaste. I'd fucking hated lying to her. When she explained, again, that she'd never had a one-night stand, I should've let her walk away, yet I was selfish and couldn't bear the thought of not having her, even if it was for one night. Just being in her presence had changed me; I'd needed her in a way I'd never needed anything in my whole life.

"Ghost?"

"Yeah, Princess?"

"The capsule is here."

I'd been so lost in thought I hadn't noticed the doors were open, waiting for us to enter. We walked into the large area, and I pulled her to the far end of the glass enclosure. Placing her in front of me, I stepped behind, caging her in. My hands covering hers on the railing, I moved to get closer still. With her back pressed against my chest, I finally let go of the breath I'd been holding.

There were times when I thought about how close I'd come to never seeing her again and my heart physically ached. Maybe I was getting sentimental, or maybe when a man finds the love of a good woman the thought of it being taken away is too much to bear.

"You okay?" Rayne asked.

"Perfect." I brushed her hair over her shoulder and leaned in to kiss her neck. "Absolutely perfect."

"What are you thinking about?"

The capsule jolted and started to move, causing her to sway in my arms.

"I was thinking about how much I love you." Then quickly added, "And him, too." I moved my hand to her still-flat belly, holding it there, wishing she was already round with our child.

"Him, huh?"

"It's a boy," I announced.

"I think it's a little early to tell. It could be a girl."

"No way would I be cursed with a girl."

"Hey! That's not nice. You wouldn't be happy if we had a girl?"

"Princess, I'd go prematurely gray if we had a daughter as smart, funny, and beautiful as you. Not to mention we'd have to buy stock in Remington because the amount of money I'd need to spend on guns and ammo to keep teenage boys away from our house would be ungodly."

"You're crazy. So, you'd rather have crazed teenage girls banging down our door trying to get to our smart, handsome, athletic son?"

"Well, yeah. How bad could that be?"

"You know nothing about teenage girls, do you?"

The capsule was almost to the top as I thought back to when I was a teenager. She wasn't wrong. The girls had been bold, doing things their fathers would've gone ballistic over.

"I'll teach him to respect women and himself. How to care for her heart and be a good man."

Rayne turned in my arms to face me.

"I know you will. And if we have a girl, you'll show her how a man should treat her. You'll teach her how to protect herself and not to settle for anything but the best." Rayne lifted her hand to my face and, just as she'd done hundreds of times, stared up at me with blinding loyalty and love.

"Goddamn right, I will." The thought of some

pimply faced boy trying to take advantage of my daughter made me see red.

"So, either way, boy or girl, this baby will be loved and protected."

I mirrored her movement and brought both my hands to her face, holding her where I wanted as I leaned down for an all too brief kiss. As much as I'd love nothing more than to make out with Rayne, this wasn't the time. I wanted her to enjoy the sights from the top of the eye. I pulled back and broke the kiss but didn't let go. "I know I keep saying this, but you've made me the happiest man on the planet. You, the baby, our family, I promise I will never stop loving you. I will never stop being thankful. I will never stop providing for you. Until my dying breath, it will always be you."

"Only you, Ghost."

Fuck, how did I get so lucky? I could barely remember a time I didn't know this kind of soul-deep love. There was before Rayne and after Rayne and everything before Rayne was bleak and dismal—a distant, unwelcome memory.

"It really is beautiful up here. How far do you think you can see?"

"On a clear day, about twenty-five miles."

"Wow. So maybe we can see Windsor Castle? It's about twenty miles away, right?"

"Maybe."

"Ghost! You're missing everything."

"No, Princess. I'm not missing a damn thing."

As much as I wanted her to take in the beauty of the city, I was content looking at my wife. Maybe Rayne was right. Maybe there was a smidge of a romantic in me after all. If being a romantic meant wanting nothing more than to lay your wife across the nearest flat surface and fuck the hell out of her until she screamed your name, then I was definitely a romantic.

7

Rayne

"I'm not gonna lie, as beautiful as the view is, I prefer my feet on the ground," I admitted to Ghost as we walked down the Queen's Walk, cutting through the Jubilee Gardens to get to the street. It wasn't so much a garden as a green space with a walkway. "I know you said just one more stop, but can we make another one before we head back?" I begged.

"Where's that?" he asked, eyeing the Park Plaza entrance just across the street from where we were.

"I want to see the Graffiti Tunnel. It's just behind the hotel."

"Come on, we need to walk a block down to Leake Street, the entrance is behind those buildings," he said.

"You know about the tunnel?"

For some reason, it stuck me as odd Ghost would

know about a tunnel featuring street artists from around the world.

"Princess, I can tell you every underground tunnel, tube station, evacuation area, where to avoid, and how to evade any terrorist threat within a thirty-mile radius. Do you think I'd take you anywhere and not have an EXFIL strategy in place?"

"Geeze, Ghost, you're not on a mission, you're on your honeymoon," I reminded him.

"You're wrong. When you're with me, I'm always on a mission."

"Okay, Rambo, let's go look at some graffiti."

He chuckled and we walked to the entrance of the tunnel; he, as always, tucked me close, making sure he was on the street side.

"Wow. I've seen pictures on the internet, but I never imagined it would be so colorful."

There was graffiti everywhere; you couldn't see a speck of the original brick wall. We walked farther in, and there was everything from words tagged on the walls to lifelike faces, even beautiful flowers. It was amazing.

We stopped to admire a stunning portrait of a black-haired woman with tears leaking out of the corner of one eye, her hands were clasped together by her face with the word hate spelled out over her fingers. It was poignant and sad in the most profound way.

"Some of the art down here should be showcased in a gallery," Ghost commented.

"I agree."

We continued down the alley, stopping to watch an artist spray paint over a rather ugly looking green serpent.

"I wonder how an artist feels when they come back to see their work and find it's been covered over?" I whispered, not wanting to bother the man working.

"Inspired," the man said, stopping his handiwork to look over his shoulder.

"I'm sorry. I didn't mean to interrupt," I apologized to the man. His hands were covered in paint, and his clothes weren't fairing any better, even his face had color on it.

"Not interrupting. It's fabulous down here, isn't it?"

"Yes. How does it inspire you when you find your work gone?"

"This place is fluid," he started. "Ever changing beauty. It's a reminder there's always something new to create, nothing stays the same. This piece would've never come to life unless I covered this god-awful snake. Don't repeat that; no one wants to look at a slithering, green beast." The man mocked shuttered. "Is this your first time down here, mates?"

"Yes," Ghost answered.

"Aye. It's something to see."

"Would you mind?" Ghost nodded toward the box of spray cans.

"Fancy yourself an artist?"

"Not at all. I promised my wife a scavenger hunt when we come back to London for our twenty-fifth anniversary. I've been leaving our mark around the city. I thought I'd leave something here as well."

"Take what you want." The man turned back to his painting, leaving Ghost to rummage through the box.

With a can of spray paint in hand, Ghost was on a mission, finally stopping when he found a place to paint without covering something important. He knelt down and in perfect lettering wrote: Princess + Ghost.

My big, badass, Delta Force Operator husband—the romantic.

With a nod and a thank you, we returned the can of paint back to the man and moved to the exit. Once back on the street, Ghost tucked me where he wanted me and we walked back to the hotel.

"Thank you for writing our names in the tunnel. I'm kinda sad it won't be there when we come back."

"I'm not. It means I'll have the opportunity to write it again."

~

Ghost

"I'm going to take a quick shower," Rayne told me

as she rummaged through her bag, presumably to find a pair of pajamas.

"Don't bother with clothes. You won't need them."

Her lips quirked up with a small grin, and I loved the blush that bloomed across her cheeks. She'd long ago learned not to argue when I asked her not to wear clothes to bed.

"Okay, Ghost. Give a minute to clean up and I'll be right out."

The bathroom door clicked shut behind Rayne, and, unlike the first time we were in this room together, I stayed while she showered. The familiarity of the situation hit me once again as I thought about her words, *clean up*. Rayne was the first woman I'd ever contemplated figuring out a way to see again. She was clean and pure, and at that time in my life nothing else was. Of course, I'd walked away like a coward thinking I was doing the right thing. I should be on my knees thanking the good Lord he brought Rayne back to me. But that would mean I was grateful she'd been bound to a dirty bed and almost raped by a young Egyptian boy in some back assed, coming of age ceremony. I could never be thankful for that. The memory of her bloodied wrists and ankles shackled to the bed turned me positively murderous. I'd carried her out of that hell hole, and she'd explained he was going to rape her seven times, and if she didn't orgasm, the process would begin again. I wasn't a vengeful man, but as I held a semi-conscious Rayne in my arms and fled the building, I'd wished I would've made the boy's death more painful.

The sound of the shower stopped, and I quickly shook the memories away. I had new memories to make with Rayne, and they wouldn't be sullied by the past. I needn't have worried; the moment Rayne stepped out of the steamy bathroom, a towel wrapped around her sexy body, and one in her hands, wringing the water from her pretty, chestnut hair all I could think about was licking the remaining water droplets from her flesh.

Feeling especially needy I stalked toward her, disrobing as I went. By the time I was in front of her, I was fully nude. With a tug on the towel, it joined my clothes on the floor, and Rayne stood completely bare.

"Fuck, you are so beautiful." The blush that covered her cheeks was sexy as hell. It didn't matter how many times we'd been together this way, she was still shy and reserved. That was until I worked her up into a frenzy, then she turned into a sexy temptress. "Remember what I told you I wanted to do to you?" I waited until she nodded. "I'm hungry, Princess." I tugged her to the bed and the second towel was discarded as she climbed on, lying in the middle on the king-sized bed. "Fucking starved, as a matter of fact."

I didn't wait for her response or for her to get better

situated; I had to have her with a need that burned. I pushed her thighs apart, kissing the soft skin, slowly making my way to her center. The first swipe of my tongue over her slit had my cock twitching in excitement. By the time I had her clit between my lips, I was willing myself not to come on the sheets.

"Ghost!" Her sweet moan filled my ears and made me smile.

"Stop teasing me."

Her plea had me slowing my movements. Even though slowing was something close to agony for my cock, I knew she'd come that much harder when I finally pushed her over the edge.

I licked and sucked and nibbled all the while Rayne's hips bucked, trying to get me to hurry.

"I'm gonna die. You're killing me. Please," she groaned.

"Dying, huh?" I lifted my head to see her watching me.

"Yes!"

"Reach down and hold your legs apart for me."

Once she had her hands where I wanted them, I teased her entrance with the tip of my finger. "Is this what you need?" I asked and pushed my finger inside.

"Yes, more," she begged. I pulled my finger out, added another, and quickly pumped them in and out.

"This enough?"

"No. I need your mouth, too."

"Where, Princess? Where do you want my mouth?"

"On my clit, Ghost. Hurry."

I did as she asked and tongued her clit, never slowing my fingers.

"Holy shit."

I found the spot I knew would drive her crazy and relentlessly rubbed, adding more pressure to her sensitive clit.

"I'm gonna—" She didn't finish her sentence before she screamed her pleasure. Wetness gushed over my hand, spilling onto the sheets. Filling my chest with some sort of Neanderthal pride.

"Up you go." I sat up on my knees, my cock relieved it wasn't being smothered between my stomach and the bed any longer. I twisted her body, bringing her up to her knees, pushing her upper body to lay flat on the bed. She was perfectly exposed in that position. Without further warning, I lined myself up and in a single thrust I was fully inside.

Fucking heaven.

I looked down at her tattoo and ran my hands over the eagle, admiring the beauty of the large bird. Wing tip to wing tip it covered her lower back. Next, I traced Big Ben, then the ghost floating around the clock tower. Quiet Professionalism in beautiful script reminded me of our cosmic connection. Even before she *knew* what my job was, she understood. The tattoo in its entirety was a sign. One I knew then and chose to ignore, and one I now recognized and would never forget—Rayne was a gift. My gift. Made perfectly for me. And me for her. I couldn't say I'd ever believed in soulmates before Rayne, but looking at the tattoo on her back there was no denying it. It might as well have been a huge neon sign flashing the word Ghost's.

Rayne's ass wiggled, urging me to move.

"Impatient little thing, aren't you?" I gripped her hips to keep her still.

"You always do that. You've seen it a thousand times. It's a tattoo. Please fuck me."

She was right, I always paused to pay homage to the mark, and it never failed to stiffen my cock when I caught a glimpse of it.

"Your wish is my command, Princess. You better brace; this is gonna be hard."

"Do it, Ghost. Fuck me."

I set a bruising pace, my thrusts making her ass ripple every time I bottomed out. She had no idea her dirty words drove me crazy. She was so classy and proper outside of the bedroom, no one would believe my wife had such a foul mouth in the sack. She was perfect.

"Reach down and rub your clit, Rayne," I demanded.

Her hand snaked down between her legs, but instead of doing what I'd asked she cupped my balls and gently rolled them.

"Holy fuck." In an effort to delay my orgasm, I closed my eyes as I pounded into her. She was tight and wet, and I was ready to come. It was obvious the little minx wasn't going to do as I wanted so I moved one hand around her hip. Gathering wetness from her soaked pussy, I went to work manipulating her clit. My other hand left her waist and I slid it under her, cupping her breast. "Lift up." She did, giving me better access. Finding her nipple, I pinched and rolled it between my fingers until I felt her pussy flutter.

"I'm gonna come, Ghost," she unnecessarily warned. She tightened her grip on my balls, giving them a firm tug, and I swear I saw stars.

"Jesus," I moaned.

"You like when I play with your balls?"

"Fuck yes."

In a wild frenzy toward completion we both continued to rub and pinch, all the while the sound of our bodies slapping together provided the perfect soundtrack. Just when I thought I was going to have to come without her, her pussy convulsed and tightened around my shaft.

"Ghost!" she shouted and the extra wetness from her orgasm coated my cock. Heat started at the base of my spine, traveling outward until my body was consumed. With one last, hard thrust I planted deep, ropes of pleasure coursed through me as I came in a rush of euphoria.

"I think you were trying to kill me," I murmured.

"What fun would that be? I still haven't had my turn tasting you."

There had been no other woman, at any time in my life, that could make me come as hard as Rayne did, then two seconds later make me bust a gut laughing.

"I don't know what's so funny. You said I could have whatever I wanted."

"Give a guy five minutes for recovery."

"Let's split the difference. I'll give you two point five. Now roll over, super-spy. I want to clean you up."

Rayne took advantage of my renewed laughter and moved, dislodging my cock, causing our combined come to run down her thigh and drip onto the bed. The sight sobered me, and once again I felt my cock stirring.

"Well, well, it doesn't look like you'll need the time after all. Lie back and let me take care of you now."

I did as she said, and a heartbeat later Rayne had her sweet lips wrapped around my rapidly hardening cock.

"Whoa." I tossed my head back when she pushed my cock to the back of her throat.

Up and down she went until I was fully erect. Her hand joined her mouth and squeezed the root, adding a twist on every down stroke; before long I was ready to blow.

"Princess," I moaned. "If you don't slow down,

this is gonna be over fast." She didn't slow. As a matter of fact, she sped up. Her hand followed her mouth up, adding a constant pressure around my cock, until she neared the tip and paused, swirling her tongue. "Holy shit. So good." My praise spurred her on, and down she went. I lost her hand but gained the added benefit of her throat swallowing around the tip of my dick and that was all it took; I shot off in her mouth. Rayne continued to suck me dry. After a few slow, gentle glides of her tongue, she pulled off and wiped her mouth with the back of her hand. I wasn't sure if that was the cutest thing I'd ever seen or the most erotic. Either way, nothing compared to the beautiful smile gracing her pretty face.

"You're pretty satisfied with yourself, aren't you?"

"Any time I can make you come in under ten minutes, I consider it a win," she replied.

"Why's that, Princess?"

"Because I know you're enjoying it."

"Well, if that's what you're gauging it by, I hate to tell you this, but two minutes with your sexy mouth latched around my cock and I'm ready to come. I spend the next eight minutes willing myself not to come so I can enjoy watching you give me head."

I tried not to laugh when she tossed a pillow at me.

"Cold?" I asked when she shivered.

"A little."

"Open my bag. On the top, there's something for you to sleep in."

She slid off the bed and padded over to my open bag on top of the dresser. Unfortunately, it didn't take her long to find what she was looking for, and she turned before I was done staring at her stunning ass.

"This?" She held up a black tank top and a pair of bright purple sleep pants.

"Yep."

"Why do you have these? I tossed them in the Goodwill pile last year." She inspected her old garments and waited for me to answer.

"I pulled them out."

"Why?"

I didn't have a good answer. I only knew when I saw them in the pile to be given away I couldn't bear to part with them.

"I don't know." I tried to blow off answering. "Hurry and come back to bed."

"In these? You want me to wear old sleep pants and not something sexy and pretty? It's our honeymoon. I thought I was supposed to wear lingerie or something."

"You look sexy in anything. Now hurry up, woman!"

"Not until you explain to me why in the world you saved these ugly, purple pants."

She wasn't going to let this go and at the risk of

sounding like a complete pussy, I had to tell her why I wanted her to wear those specific pajamas before my wife would get into bed so we could go to sleep.

"Because the first night we were together, you wore that black tank top and those purple pants. I remember thinking how beautiful you were. You weren't trying to look sexy or flirty—you were just being you. And I'd never, in all my life, felt so at ease. We lay in this bed." I patted the mattress under me. "And discovered each other for the first time. You, in those pajamas. I didn't want them thrown away."

The smile that appeared would've knocked me on my ass if I hadn't been lying in bed.

"Thank you."

"For what?"

"For being my prince. My fairytale. Everything I ever wanted in a partner. And for being—dare I say it—the most wonderful, dreamy husband a girl could ever hope for."

"You're a nut. Put those awful pants on and get your fine ass back to bed. We have a long day tomorrow and I don't want you to be tired."

"Oh, all right, Mr. Bossy Pants."

"I'll show you bossy, Rayne."

"Sure you will, Captain."

Not for the first time that night Rayne had me roaring with laughter. Goddamn, she was the world's most perfect woman.

8

Rayne

“Oh my gosh, it’s . . . wow.” I looked around the central lobby of The Palace of Westminster—better known to us yanks as The House of Parliament—and was in awe. The vaulted ceiling looked to be fifty feet high with gold everywhere. There were no words to describe the chandelier that hung high above our heads.

“It’s pretty impressive,” Ghost said, taking in the sights as well.

“What are those?” I pointed to one of the four, very large designs above each archway.

“Each of the mosaic panels represent the Patron Saint for each of the four countries that make up the United Kingdom. England, Wales, Northern Ireland, and Scotland.”

"And what are the statues that surround the archways?"

"Those are the Kings and Queens from England and Scotland. I believe starting from Edward the First going forward."

"I bet this tile floor is hard to keep dry with all the rain they have here. It has to be an accident waiting to happen."

"Come on, Princess, there's someone I want you to meet."

Ghost tugged my hand, and I reluctantly followed. I could've stood in the middle of the lobby, spinning in circles, all day and still couldn't have absorbed all of the beauty and history in the room.

Standing off to the side of the reception desk was a very large man dressed in a black suit. His scowl turned into a smile as we approached.

"Sparky," Ghost said, stopping in front of the man and offered his hand.

The man chuckled before he grabbed Ghost's hand, shaking vigorously and pulling him in for a man hug, complete with a hard slap on the back.

"Ghost. Good to see you, mate."

"Oliver, this is my wife, Rayne."

"A pleasure to meet the woman who can put up with this here, bloke."

"Nice to meet you, Oliver."

"If you two are finished looking around the Central Lobby, we'll start our tour."

"Tour?" I looked to Ghost, then around the area and didn't see any people gathered around waiting. "Do we have tickets?"

"No ticket needed for our tour, ma'am."

"Oliver's gonna give us a special, behind-the-scenes tour. I thought you might like to see the Chamber rooms."

"Oh my God, yes. Are we allowed, or are you bribing people again?"

Oliver chuckled before he answered for Ghost. "Not exactly. He's calling in favors, if you will."

"I would love the super-secret tour if you're not going to get in trouble."

Both men laughed, and Ghost shook his head before leaning down, giving me a sweet peck on my cheek. "Princess, it is very unlikely Oliver *can* get into trouble. He has friends in high places."

"Oh, so, your brethren then."

"Something like that. Come on, let's take a look around."

We followed Oliver through one of the archways into a wide hallway.

"This is the Common's Corridor. If you turn around and look back toward the lobby, the doorway directly opposite of where we are, is the Peer's Corridor. That side of the octagon is The House of Lords. The Prince's

Chamber is also on that side. As well as Victoria Tower and the Royal Entrance."

Oliver stopped to allow us to look at some large murals painted on the walls. Four on each side, all with very interesting names. I stood in front of one titled: *The Executioner*.

"Stunning artwork," I noted.

"Not up to my tastes," Oliver commented. "A bit stuffy if you ask me."

He wasn't wrong, however the history behind the paintings made them beautiful.

"This is the Common's Lobby. You can see it's quite a large space for nothing more than mailboxes for the MP's and a gathering place. That, over there, is where the agenda, committee notes, and whatnot can be picked up."

This area wasn't as grand as the Central Lobby; however the intricate stonework and statues were still impressive.

Oliver didn't give us long to look around before he started walking again. Marble flooring gave way to green carpet and stone walls into dark, wooden panels that were polished to a high sheen. There were several doors on either side of us, however Oliver continued to walk straight through a set of double doors.

"And this is the House of Commons Chamber."

"Holy wow. Really?"

Ghost squeezed my hand before he let go so I could explore on my own.

The ceiling in there had to be at least three stories tall. There was a U-shaped balcony, giving anyone standing or sitting up there the perfect view to peek in on whatever debate was taking place below them.

"Why are there red lines on the floor?" I asked.

"Members may not speak from the Chamber floor. They have to remain behind the red line," Ghost answered.

"And this?" I pointed to a large, wooden structure in the middle of the room holding books and two large brackets that looks like they were meant to display something.

"The mace is placed there when the Chamber is in session. It is a five foot long ornamental club," Oliver explained. "It's carried in each time the House is sitting."

"Everything's green in here," I noted, looking at the stadium style seating. All the benches were upholstered in a deep, leafy color, and the carpet was a more muted hue.

"The color of the commoner, one can assume, but it's not known for certain why the color was chosen. However, the House of Lords is red, the color of nobility. Are you ready to continue?" Oliver asked.

"Yes, sorry. I hope I'm not asking too many questions. Everything's so interesting."

"Not at all."

Ghost walked beside me and clasped my hand in his, drawing me to a stop. "Are you enjoying yourself?"

"Are you kidding me? Our own personal tour. This is the best day ever."

"I'm glad you like it. There's more to see."

We continued through the Chamber, exiting through another hallway on the far side of where we'd entered. It shined with the same polished, dark wooden paneling. The corridors back there were less impressive than the ones on the other side of the House of Commons Chamber. More utilitarian, leading to what looked like janitorial closets and storage. Nothing particularly fancy or pretty.

The hall came to an end, and Oliver stopped in front of a closed door. I looked around, trying to figure out where we were going when I finally saw it.

"Are you serious?" I gasped and turned to Ghost. He smiled at me and nodded. "How? No way! Really?"

I knew I was squealing like a three-year-old hopped up on Twizzlers and Pixy Stix and if Oliver wasn't there, I may have danced a jig.

I'd lost focus on everything around me except the one thing I was most excited about, a sign saying Clock Tower.

Oliver unlocked the door and held it open for us.

"Ghost," I whispered. The reality of the situation

breaking through my excitement. "Are we really going to the top?"

"Yeah, Princess. Are you up for all these stairs? All 334 of them."

I was going to climb the clock tower stairs. A once in a lifetime opportunity.

"I'm ready."

The staircase was small and circular. It was a stark contrast to the rest of the building; there was nothing grand about the trek up.

"Are you counting?" Ghost asked from behind me.

"Yes. Don't talk or you'll make me lose my place." I peered over the railing and, though we were only seventy-five steps into our journey, it appeared we'd climbed quite a distance, but when I looked up, the top seemed to be at least a mile away.

I didn't know how Ghost had pulled it off, but tonight he was going to get one hell of a thank you.

Ghost

Watching Rayne's eyes light up with excitement was worth every bit of juggling I'd had to do to get her access to the Clock Tower. I still had a few more surprises for my wife and I couldn't wait to show her.

"What's this?" she asked, pointing to an open room.

"The Prison Room. Once upon a time, this room

was used as a prison for unruly members of Parliament. After a few nights locked away up here they tended to behave." Oliver chuckled. "Now it's simply a museum of sorts."

"May I?" she asked and motioned to the room.

"Of course, take your time. We still have over 200 steps to go."

Rayne disappeared into the room, leaving Oliver and I alone on the landing.

"Congratulations. You look happy."

"Thanks, man, I am."

"She doesn't know, does she?" he asked and gestured up the stairs.

"No. She didn't know she'd get to see Big Ben either. I told her we were coming here so she could get a postcard. She's been collecting them whenever we stop and mailing them to her girls back home."

"I heard all of you were married off. Even Truck."

"Yeah, the fucker's been married awhile now. He and Mary tied the knot and didn't tell anyone about it."

"Damn, bet that hurt."

"It caused some issues, but we're straight now, so it's all good. What about you, Sparky? You got a woman locked away somewhere?"

"I have many women in many places, but nothing like you have. Don't have time with my schedule." There was a sadness in Oliver's gaze that was familiar.

I'd had the same look when I'd met Rayne then left her. For six months, I'd walked around in a haze.

"Make time. Trust me; it's worth it."

"What's worth what?" Rayne appeared in the doorway. "It's really cool in there. Ghost, you wanna look around?"

"I've been in there before, Princess. If you're done, let's go up."

"I knew it." She walked to my side and looked up, smiling. "I knew you'd been up here before."

Oliver laughed and shook his head. "I bet Ghost has been a lot of places most people would only dream of seeing."

"I know you're right. I don't bother to ask because I know he can't tell me, but I'm sure I'd be amazed."

The rest of the walk was done in silence. Rayne was counting steps and I was thinking about some of the places I'd been; most were shit holes. I'd spent a lot of time in the desert, dirty, hot, and hungry. However, I had to admit there were some places I'd been to most people didn't even know existed. Vaults deep underground, fallout shelters for the US government, and evacuation tunnels. Not that any of those things would interest Rayne.

"Wow, there are a lot of steps," Rayne commented, sounding a little out of breath.

"We're almost to the clock dial. How are you holding up?"

"Great. It's a good thing I'm in shape."

"I'll carry you down if you need me to."

"I'm sure you would. But there's no need. I promise, I feel fine."

A few more turns and the winding staircase ended. Oliver opened the door and allowed Rayne to proceed him, following her in.

"This is the clock dial." Oliver pointed out. "Each of the four faces has 312 cut opal glass panels set in cast iron. Behind you, on the wall, there are twenty-eight bulbs to illuminate the clock face. Each of the four have them."

"Holy wow, it's so big."

"Twenty-three feet in diameter," Oliver explained.

We walked around and looked at all four faces before climbing another set of stairs and entering the room above the clock dial.

"This is the Link Room where the actual clock is housed. The going train, the chiming train, and the striking train." Oliver pointed out each moving piece of the clock. "And of course, the escapement and pendulum."

"I had no idea there were so many gears." Rayne moved closer for a better look. "Why are there coins on the pendulum?'

"The clock keeper adds and removes pennies to keep the clock in perfect time. Remove a penny to slow down, add a penny to speed it up."

"You ready to see Big Ben?" I asked.

"Yes!"

"Just a few more steps up to the belfry." Oliver walked back to the door and waited for us to follow.

"Three hundred and thirty-four," Rayne announced when she took the last step onto the landing. "Holy shit. That's Big Ben!" Rayne rushed into the room before I could stop her.

Ten steps in she came to halt, causing me to nearly knock her over in my quest to stop her and warn her of my last surprise.

"Ghost," she whispered. "Is that? Is that um . . ."

"Ghost! You finally made it, mate."

9

Rayne

My eyes must've been playing tricks on me. It had to be the altitude and dehydration.

"Your Royal Highness. Or is it Duke now? I could never keep all your titles straight." Ghost stopped and looked over at the beautiful brunette standing in front of us. "May I?" The man nodded, and Ghost continued, "Your Royal Highness. It's a pleasure to see you again."

Ghost placed his arm around my waist, preventing me from swaying on my feet. What in the world was happening?

"This is my wife, Rayne. Rayne, this is Spike Wells and his beautiful wife, Meghan. The Duke and Duchess of Sussex," Ghost unnecessarily announced.

I wasn't sure why Ghost was calling Prince Harry that silly name, but anyone with a television or the internet would know who the couple was. Hell, I remember watching the man grow up and had read the tabloid headlines about him.

I was at a loss. I wanted to kill Ghost. Did I bow or curtsy? Was I allowed to speak to them? Thankfully, the woman stepped forward and extended her hand.

"Very nice to meet you, Rayne. Please call me Meghan."

I took her hand, relieved she was so kind. "It's a pleasure to meet you. I apologize, I'm a little shocked to see you both. I'm afraid I wasn't told we'd be meeting you or I would've dressed for the occasion and possibly brushed up on royal protocol."

Meghan didn't let go of my hand and tugged me away from Ghost.

"Don't be silly. I've had hours of training and I still get confused. Up here, away from prying eyes, we are simply Harry and Meghan. It is nice to be normal every once in a while."

That was so nice of her.

"Thank you."

"So, Rayne, did you enjoy your walk up the tower?" the prince asked.

I hoped like hell I wasn't blushing. Now that Meghan had released my hand, I clasped both in front of me to mask how badly I was shaking.

"I did. This is amazing."

"It truly is. Was Oliver helpful in answering all of your questions?"

"He was. Thank you for allowing me to see such a wonderful treasure."

"It's the least I could do for the man who saved my life."

Ghost had saved the prince's life?

"I think you're overstating the situation, Spike," Ghost chimed in. He always did that—downplayed his heroic efforts.

"Don't let this bloke fool you. We were pinned down by the Taliban, almost completely surrounded. We'd called in an airstrike and, seemingly out of nowhere, Ghost, Truck, Beatle, Blade, Fletch, Coach, and Hollywood came up on our position. At the time, none of them knew my identity. I was commanding a troop of eleven men. I kept most of my face covered at all times, not wanting to be recognized. Ghost and his team held off the advancing Taliban, and we were able to fall back to safety. It was a good thing, too; the airstrike had been delayed. If it weren't for the team, we all would've been dead. Oliver, over there, included."

"Wow. I had no idea."

"It wasn't until we were back on post debriefing when the team found out who I was. Even then, none of them treated me as anything more than a fellow soldier. No one cared I was in line for the throne. I was Spike Wells, nothing more. I am forever in their debt."

"There's no debt, Spike. You're just lucky we were nearby and could save your sorry asses."

"Ghost! You can't call the prince a sorry ass," I chided.

The men in the room chuckled, and Meghan smiled.

"I believe Ghost can call him whatever he wants. Besides it's good for His Royal Highness; it keeps him down to earth with the rest of us common folk."

"Is that so, cheeky woman? Are you saying I have an inflated ego?" the prince asked, grabbing a squealing Meghan around the waist, pulling her close.

"I would never." She giggled.

"I think you would." After a smoldering kiss, which was surely against royal standards, he let her go. "So, what do you think of Big Ben here?"

"I think it's amazing."

"It's too bad the unsightly scaffolding is up. The view from up here is normally spectacular."

"I'm sure it is. When will the bell ring again?"

"Not for a bit, I'm afraid. There's much to repair."

"Well, it's wonderful to see all the same. I really can't thank you enough for allowing me to see the famous Big Ben. This is something I'll never forget."

"Did you look around the Prison Room on your way up?" Meghan asked.

"I did. I can't believe I never knew the tower was used as a prison."

"Crazy how much history is all around you," Meghan commented.

I wanted to pinch myself to see if I was dreaming. There I was, standing in the belfry, next to the most famous bell in the world having a normal conversation with a prince and the . . . I wasn't sure what her official title was . . . duchess? Princess? Her Royal Highness? The five of us chatting like it was no big deal. And, Ghost, I had a million questions for him about saving the prince. I knew I wasn't allowed to ask, but I was dying to know more about the rescue.

"Are you ready for lunch?" Prince Harry asked.

"Lunch?"

"You haven't told her of our plans?" He turned to Ghost.

"No. I thought it would be more exciting to let the day play out. Seeing the wonder light her face as each new surprise is revealed has been the highlight of my day."

"Isn't that romantic?" Meghan said, elbowing the prince's side.

"Romantic? I took us to Botswana to camp under the stars. All he did was show her an old clock bell," he joked.

"No, not an old clock. He's given me the fairytale. Shown me things I could only dream of seeing." I turned to Ghost and rolled up on my toes, kissing his cheek. "Thank you for this."

"I'm glad you like it, Princess." The reddish tinge on Ghost's cheeks told me he wasn't unaffected by my words, and when he leaned down to whisper in my ear, he confirmed my suspicion. "If we were alone up here, I'd find a place to lay you down and show you just how much I love you."

Without meaning to, I looked around the belfry trying to scout out a location we could've used. There was nothing in the big room but a high bell in the center and concrete floors.

"I don't think that would've worked," I noted.

"I can make anything work." He chuckled.

"Are we ready, lovebirds? Tea begins in an hour," Harry said, reminding us we were getting ready to leave.

"One more thing." Ghost pulled out a ballpoint pen from his pocket and held it up for Prince Harry to see.

"Right. Yes, of course. We'll wait here."

Ghost took my hand and walked us round the bell where there was an intricate, hand carved door. He opened it, revealing a small utility closest.

"Here." He placed the pen in my hand. When I didn't move, he pushed the door farther open revealing the back side.

I had to blink a few times before I understood what I was seeing. "What's this?"

"Exactly what it looks like."

"Ghost! You're not thinking of adding our names to the back of this door, are you?"

I scanned the names and dates carved into the wood. The earliest one I could see dated back to 1870. In the center, there were more recent additions. Elizabeth and Philip 1947. William and Catherine 2011. Harry and Meghan 2018.

"I cannot write on this door. That's the queen's name."

"Indeed it is."

"I can't." I handed the pen back to Ghost.

He had no issue adding our names near the bottom of the door.

Princess and Ghost 2018

"There, our names are forever etched into a royal heirloom," he said proudly.

"I cannot believe you did that," I said through a fit of nervous laughter. "That is the most insane thing I've ever seen."

"I promised you a twenty-five year anniversary scavenger hunt. Now we'll have to come back." He started back to where the group was waiting for us. "We'd better hurry; we wouldn't want Spike to miss his tea," Ghost mocked.

Did that really just happen? I was truly at a loss.

"Lunch sounds great. I'm starving," I said, trying to mask my giddy satisfaction.

Harry, Meghan, and Oliver were all waiting for us near the exit by the time we came back around.

"Ready?"

"Yes. Thank you," Ghost answered.

"When we get to the bottom, we'll head out through the Royal entrance. Oliver will go with you and drive," Harry explained.

And down we went, 344 steps. I used the time to memorize every moment of this adventure; I never wanted to forget a single minute of the day.

10

Ghost

"Where are we going for lunch?" Rayne asked from the back seat.

"It's a surprise."

"I don't think I can handle any more surprises, Ghost. I feel bad I didn't get to say a proper goodbye when we parted ways with—"

"You'll see them for lunch. We're joining them."

I knew she was fishing for hints. Spike had told her we had lunch plans while in the belfry.

"Oh, that's right," she pouted. "Is that Hyde Park?"

"It is," Oliver answered. "Have you been?"

"No, never." Rayne's face was almost pressed against the window as she took in what she could from the moving vehicle.

"If you have time, you should. There are many hidden trails and gardens. It's quite lovely."

"Quite lovely? Have you gone soft, Sparky?" I poked at Oliver.

"Some of us know how to behave in front of a lady. I can be a classy bloke when I want."

"Whatever you say, friend." I laughed.

"How did you get the nickname Sparky?" Rayne asked.

"We were outside of Kabul and on one of the very few paved roads. Out of nowhere we came under attack by rebels. You see, we were in circa 1980 Toyota pickup trucks, not very comfortable, but trusty. We'd left the airstrip after picking up supplies, so the assumption was they only wanted to steal our cargo. Anyway, both of my back tires were hit and completely flat at that point, but I couldn't stop. Spike was in the truck with me and Ghost and Blade in the one behind us." I couldn't believe Oliver was telling Rayne this story. So much for keeping top-secret missions secret. "Eventually, the rubber had come free of the rim, leaving me driving at a high rate of speed on metal. All of a sudden, over the radio, this bloke starts complaining he couldn't see because of the sparks flying from the back of my truck. After that, Ghost and Blade started calling me Sparky. It caught on and Spike and the rest of my unit coined the name as well."

"Holy shit. What happened next?" Rayne asked,

obviously happy with all the new information she was getting.

"Blade, the crazy bloke, climbed out of the cab and got into the bed of the truck. He must've sprayed ten or twelve full magazines of ammo at the rebels. One of the vehicles chasing us veered off the road and hit a parked car, flipping it end over end. The other car stopped to help them."

"How did you make it back with no rear tires?"

"We ditched the truck, loaded our supplies in the back of Ghost's, and Blade and I sat in the bed. It was an uncomfortable ride."

"Was there ever a comfortable ride in Afghanistan?" I asked, remembering the shit trucks with no padding on the seats and non-existent shock absorbers.

"There was nothing comfortable about that hell-hole," Oliver answered.

Thankfully, before Rayne could ask any more questions, Oliver turned down an alley, drawing her attention to her surroundings.

Oliver slowed at the guard gate and was waved through without stopping.

"Where are we?" Rayne asked.

"Almost there, Princess."

"Ghost. Seriously. I am not dressed for a fancy restaurant. I'll die of embarrassment."

"You look beautiful. And we're not going to a restaurant."

"That sign says Kensington Gardens!" she shrieked. "As in Kensington Palace?"

"One and the same."

"Oh, put the poor woman out of her misery and tell her," Oliver said, pulling the car through another set of guarded gates.

Oliver slowly pulled through and the black, ornate iron gates, complete with gold leaf tips, and the OS14 Royal Protection Officers closed them behind us as soon as we passed.

Rayne's head was swiveling back and forth, looking for any hint of where she might be. I was pleased she wasn't familiar with the Kensington Palace grounds.

Spike stepped into view along with his new bride, both smiling and holding hands. I was thrilled my old friend had found the same happiness I had.

Oliver exited the car and opened Rayne's door, offering his hand to help her out.

"Ma'am," he said with a small bow once she was steady on her feet.

"Are you hitting on my wife?" I joked.

"She is a stunning morsel; however, I prefer my women unattached."

"Morsel? Jesus, where do you come up with your pickup lines? No wonder you're single. Now hand over my woman."

"Welcome," Spike greeted. "Thank you for agreeing to have lunch here. Nothing ruins a meal more than photographers."

"Ghost?" Rayne tugged on my shirt, stopping me from following the prince. "Is this Nottingham Cottage?"

"It is."

"But—"

"Princess. This is nothing more than Spike's home. Relax and enjoy yourself. It's just like having a barbecue at Fletch's."

"You're joking, right?"

"Relax."

This was not going as planned. I wanted Rayne to have fun, not be stiff and freaked out. Maybe this had been a bad idea.

"You're right. I'm being stupid. They're just people." She smiled, then muttered, "Everyday, royal people."

"I hope you don't mind, I asked the staff to set a table in the garden," Meghan said as we entered. "Would you like a tour before lunch?" she asked Rayne.

"Would you mind? I don't want to impose. This is your home."

"Not at all. Let's let the men reminisce about their glory days." Meghan smiled and motioned for Rayne to follow.

Spike and I both stood, waiting for the women to leave before he offered us a seat.

"My apologies we missed the wedding. The team was called away on a mission. I was happy I'd never told Rayne about the invitation; she would've been crushed if she'd known. She did, however, watch it live on TV with the rest of the women. I heard so much about it, I feel as if I was there in person."

"I wish I could've taken her to an island and done it in private. There are some things a man wants to share with just his bride." There was a longing in his voice. I couldn't imagine always being in the spotlight, having my every move criticized and documented.

I understood why he'd spent as long as he had in Afghanistan. There, he was Spike Wells, troop leader, not the sixth in line for the throne. The news outlets have reported he's done two tours, however that's inaccurate. He's done more than two tours, and his time in country had been downplayed as well.

"So, tell me, how are the rest of the guys? Truck did email with an update, but he always leaves out the gossip."

Oliver joined us, setting a tray with three crystal tumblers and a decanter of amber liquid down on the table in front of us.

"Good idea. Let's toast," Spike said, pouring each of us two fingers of Scottish whisky. "To best mates."

Rayne

Lunch had turned into dinner, and while I was still amazed I'd spent the day with royalty, Ghost had been right; as soon as I'd relaxed, I had a great time. The prince was hilarious. Of course, like any good American royal watcher, I'd read the tabloid stories about his exploits. I wasn't sure if I was happy or disappointed to learn much of the bad-boy prince stories that had been printed were greatly exaggerated. He was caring and down to earth and positively in love with his wife.

We talked about everything from his charity work to more stories about Afghanistan. Harry even explained why Ghost called him Spike Wells. Who knew, both Prince William and Harry had used code names when they were in college. Prince William was known plainly as Steve, and Prince Harry, being the rebel, chose the name Spike. But what really got him animated and happy was when he spoke about his time in Africa. I was honored when he pulled out his laptop and shared his personal photo collection. The couple planned on spending more time there in the near future. And when they'd invited Ghost and me to come along, I nearly swallowed my tongue.

Meghan and I finished cleaning up the dinner dishes. Yes, Her Royal Highness did dishes. She'd insisted on us cooking and not calling in the staff, explaining she and Spike enjoyed doing normal, everyday things together. Now we were gathered in the living room. The men were enjoying an after-dinner whisky when Oliver offered to pour me a drink.

"No, thank you," I refused.

He held an empty glass in Meghan's direction and she, too, declined. I'd noticed, like me, she opted for water with dinner as well.

"What's wrong with the women tonight? Are you both up the duff or something?"

Meghan's eyes widened in shock, and Ghost stiffened beside me. I searched my brain trying to decode the British slang but couldn't remember what it meant.

"You know, a bun in the oven, in the family way, or as you Americans so eloquently put it—knocked up," Oliver helpfully continued.

"Um . . ." I looked to Ghost, waiting for him to respond. We'd decided to wait until everyone was back from their honeymoons to announce our pregnancy to our friends.

"I cannot confirm nor deny that intel," Ghost told the room.

"Cheeky bastard." Oliver laughed. "Congratulations."

All eyes turned to Spike. If the broad smile of his face and the pretty blush on Meghan's cheeks were anything to go by, I'd say she was pregnant as well.

"I, too, cannot confirm nor deny. You'll have to stay tuned and see if an official announcement is made."

Oliver sat back and crossed his arms over his chest. "Just great. Now babysitting will be added to my official duties. I don't wipe arses."

The conversation flowed, and as we were getting ready to leave, Harry turned to me and asked, "Did you have a good day?"

"The best. I really can't thank you enough. I've learned so much, too."

"Before you leave, do you have any other questions?" he offered.

"There is one thing. But it's personal and probably rude of me to ask."

I twisted my hands together. There was one thing I was dying to know. I could've looked it up on the internet but if the prince was offering to answer questions, I might as well get the answer straight from the horse's mouth, so to speak.

"And?"

"What's your last name?"

Laughter filled the room until Meghan cut in. "I don't know what's funny. I had the same question, too."

"My Christian name is Henry Charles Albert David. Quite a mouthful. We do not use surnames. However, I come from the House of Windsor. If you're asking what's on my passport and foreign documents that require a surname, it's Mountbatten-Windsor. My grandfather's surname hyphenated with my grandmother's family name."

"How do you sign documents if you don't use a surname?"

"My first name only," he answered.

"Thank you for answering my silly question."

"I told you there was a lot for me to learn," Meghan added.

We said our goodbyes and Meghan pulled me in for a hug and slipped her personal email address into my hand before we headed to the car. Oliver was going to drive us to the hotel before returning to Nottingham Cottage for the evening. I'd also learned that Oliver was Spike's personal protection guard. It was something similar to the president's Secret Service agents. All the royals had a Royalty Protection Group around them at all times, and Personal and Close Protection Officers when they were in public. Oliver only guarded the couple and was close friends with both.

"I love it here," I said as I watched the city's lights twinkle from the back seat. "So much history," I said dreamily.

"You should visit more often," Oliver said.

"I wish."

I did what sightseeing I could as we sped down the road. Oliver, obviously knowing his way around the city, avoided all the congested tourist areas. Before I knew it, we were pulling up in front of the Park Plaza.

After thank yous and handshakes, Ghost and I were alone in the elevator.

"I can't wait to tell Mary about our day." Ghost chuckled and tucked me close. "Thank you."

"You're welcome, Princess. I hope you enjoyed it."

"Enjoyed it? There are no words."

"Good."

"I'll have to show you how grateful I am."

"Show me?" Ghost cocked his head to the side in question.

"Oh, yeah. Show you. Tonight, I'm first." I crooked my finger at him, and he leaned down, allowing me to whisper in his ear. "First, I'm going to drive you crazy with my mouth, and then I'm going to climb on top of you and do that thing with my hips you like. And after that, I'm going to ride reverse cowgirl so you can watch my tattoo as I get us both off," I whispered.

"Princess," he growled.

"Yeah, Ghost?"

"One change. Before you ride me, you're gonna crawl up and sit on my face so I can tongue your sweet pussy. Then you can do that thing with your hips I love so much."

"Anything you want, Ghost."

11

Rayne

"What did you think of the Tower of London? Is it all you'd dreamed it'd be?" Ghost asked as we wandered the courtyard of the infamous fortress.

"I could spend all day here and not get bored. There's so much to learn. I wish I hadn't forgotten my cell phone at the hotel, I could've FaceTimed Emily. She would've loved seeing the Crown Jewels. Did you see that 530 carat diamond?"

As interesting as the Tower had been, nothing would ever come close to seeing Big Ben. Even twenty-four hours later, I couldn't stop thinking about how much fun we'd had.

"Not exactly the basement torture chamber you thought it would be?"

"No, but poor Queen Anne Boleyn was executed on the lawn."

"She seemed to have made many enemies during her three years as queen."

"It wasn't her fault. King Henry seemed to have had an issue keeping it in his pants. That man wrote love letters to any woman who struck his fancy. He was a cheater and weak minded. Even if she was the schemer historians make her out to be, he didn't have to follow along."

The beauty of the day wasn't lost on me. We'd gotten lucky, and there wasn't a cloud in sight; the blue sky made an amazing backdrop for the stone castle. So much wealth and antiquity were hidden behind these walls. "I bet it's beautiful at night, all lit up."

"You know, we could come back one evening or we could go to the Hampton Court Palace. It has been said a screaming Queen Catherine Howard runs down the great hall."

"That would be a no." I shuttered at the thought. "A big, fat no way."

A huge influx of tourists flooded the courtyard, a man with a stroller came dangerously close to knocking me over, and Ghost caught my hand and pulled me close. "Be careful, Princess, a guided tour just let out. Are you ready for lunch?"

"Before we go, I want to stop at the gift shop and look around."

"Right this way, my lady." Ghost made a grand sweeping gesture with his free hand and we began walking toward the over-priced tourist-trap the London Tower called a souvenir store.

The White Tour Shop was no less packed than the courtyard had been. Ghost was being a good sport, following me around without complaint. I had something for all the girls and was now on a quest to find Annie the perfect gift. Just when I'd thought I was going to have to give up, I stumbled upon a sword and shield.

"What about this?" I asked Ghost. "Not exactly Army, but still combat related."

"Get her the sword. Fletch will shit a brick; it's perfect."

"You're bad. But I can see Annie zooming around in her tank wielding a sword." I found the perfect-looking one on the bottom shelf. "Here, will you hold my water?"

Ghost took my bottle and stepped to the side, allowing a group of women to peruse the shelves next to me.

I pulled the sword off the shelf and examined the gold-plating and wondered if Annie would deem gold "too girly." Deciding she would, I moved farther down the aisle, finding basic pewter swords. The patina made them looked bruised and worn, as if they'd been used in a great battle. Yes, those were perfect for little Annie and the imaginary Army battalion she led.

With the sword in hand, I stood and looked around the shop.

"Ghost?"

~

Ghost

I fucking hated crowds. Too many people packed into a small space. My eyes scanned for exits and hidden doorways. There should've been a maximum occupancy of fifty fewer people than were crammed into the gift shop. I'd been watching Rayne pick through the assortment of swords for Annie when a little girl bumped into me, spilling her very large cup of lemonade. With the cup smashed between us and cool liquid running down the front of the little girl's dress and the leg of my pants, I grabbed her shoulders before she fell.

"Whoa. Are you okay?" Her eyes widened in horror, and tears sprang to her eyes. I looked around, waiting for a parent to come to my rescue, but no adults seemed to be looking for the girl. "Where's your mom?"

The girl shook her head and pinched her lips. I suppose she was doing the right thing not speaking to me, stranger danger and all that, but it was not helping find her parents.

I knelt down, ignoring the sticky, wet mess, and tried to keep a respectable distance. "My name is Ghost. You're a pretty smart girl not talking to a stranger, but we need to find your mommy and daddy. Do you see them?" She remained quiet but shook her head again. I could see panic was quickly making its way to the surface. "Okay. Would you like to stand here and wait while I walk to the checkout counter to get a police officer or would you like to walk with me?" The girl pointed to the cashier station. I took that as confirmation she wanted to come with me. With a quick glance over to find Rayne still looking through the swords, I started to walk toward the cashier with the little girl following closely.

After explaining to the frazzled employee the little girl beside me was lost, the woman informed me they didn't have a loud speaker in the shop, advising me I needed to take the girl to the security office just outside the store. The less than helpful woman didn't seem to care a man taking a child that was not his out of the safety of a public area was not acceptable and extremely dangerous. Arguing was getting me nowhere. The sooner I took the girl to the police, the faster I could get back to Rayne.

Once again, I knelt down and spoke to the child. "Are you sure you don't see your mommy or daddy in here?" She shook her head. "Did you hear what the lady said about me taking you to the office outside where the police officers are?" She nodded. "Do you want to go with me or wait here for me to bring them to you?"

"I'm scared," she finally spoke. Her wobbly voice accompanied by a fresh set of tears pissed me off. How could a parent lose their child? Being as crowded as it was, it was an abductor's dream. They'd have easy pickings, snatching a child while the parent mindlessly browsed shit to buy.

"I know you are. We'll find your parents."

I started for the exit and was happy I was the person she'd bumped into and not some lunatic looking to steal a child. She followed closely but was careful not to touch me in any way. It would've been a hell of a lot quicker if I could've picked her up and muscled my way through the throngs of patrons.

Finally outside, the security office was indeed directly next door to the shop, further pissing me the fuck off the cashier hadn't called an officer into the shop instead allowing a stranger to leave with a missing girl.

"There you are!" A woman rushed to the girl as soon as we stepped foot in the office. "Oh my God."

The crying mother got to her knees and hugged the little girl tightly. Before I could reprimand the mother for not keeping a better eye on her child, a man turned from the officer he was speaking to and saw his daughter safely in her mother's arms. The tears in the father's eyes were like a sucker punch to the gut. He'd beaten himself up more than anything I could've said would have.

"Thank you." He rushed to my side, grabbing my hand, and shaking it vigorously. "Thank you so much. Thank you."

"No problem. Glad I could help." I pulled my hand away.

Kneeling, the man joined his wife and child on the floor, wrapping them both in his arms.

Good deed done for the day, I left to go in search of my wife. I still wanted to walk across the Tower Bridge before we had lunch. Going straight to where I'd left Rayne, I hoped she was done shopping. Finding the area empty, I glanced around the shop. I walked up and down a few aisles and still couldn't find her. Trying to tamp down the panic that was quickly bubbling to the surface, I went to the front of the store for a better view. Passing the checkout counter, I saw a basket set to the side with a sword sticking up over the edge of the plastic carrier. I scanned the rest of the items, noting all the gifts Rayne had picked out for our friends.

"Excuse me, ma'am? I believe those are my wife's things back there."

The woman turned and looked before speaking. "Yes. Would you like to pay for them now?"

What the fuck?

"Why is it there?"

"She asked me to hold it. She said she needed to find you to pay for it."

Pay for it? Rayne had a wallet full of credit cards. That didn't make any sense.

"Was she alone when she left?"

A thousand scenarios played out in my head. None of them good.

"She appeared to be." The woman eyed me suspiciously. "Aren't you the man with the missing child?"

"You mean the little girl you let walk of the store with a stranger? Yes. She's next door with her parents. Now, my wife. Are you sure she was alone when she left?"

"Sir, I'm going to have to ask you to leave."

"Leave?" I growled. "Answer me. Was she alone and how long ago did she leave?"

"I think you should leave before I call security."

"Fucking brilliant. *Now* you'll call security?"

Deciding I didn't need the extra hassle of arguing with the police, I left and stood outside the gift shop looking in every direction for Rayne.

Nothing.

She was nowhere in sight.

I paced in front of the store, even went back inside to look for her again—still nothing.

I couldn't leave the general vicinity in case Rayne

came back looking for me. So, I did the only thing I could, I pulled my phone out, brought up a picture of Rayne, and showed it to every person that walked by, asking if they'd seen her.

Once an hour had passed, any hopes I'd had that Rayne was nearby, lost in the sea of tourists and I simply couldn't see her, had diminished.

Fuck.

Where are you, Rayne?

The panic I'd felt over the last hour had turned to terror. I couldn't find Rayne anywhere. More and more people had finished their tours, and the ever-changing landscape of tourists made it impossible to find her. She'd vanished.

I dialed the number of the one person I prayed could help me find Rayne.

12

Rayne

Ghost was going to be furious. I'd broken the cardinal rule for when you were separated from someone—I'd left the last place he'd seen me. After I'd found the sword I wanted, I'd stood but couldn't find him. I'd walked around the store for a minute and when I couldn't spot him, I'd stupidly asked the woman behind the counter to hold my gifts so I could go in search of him.

Why did I leave the store? So stupid.

I thought maybe he'd stepped outside to get some fresh air. He hated crowds, but I knew better than to think he'd ever leave my side when so many people were around. Well, he did leave my side; that was why I couldn't find him. Maybe if I'd used my credit card and paid for the items I would've been in the shop when he came back. Instead, I'd been a cheapskate and wanted to use his cash instead of paying the exchange rate fee the bank would charge. In hindsight, paying the extra three percent would've saved me hours of searching the Tower of London grounds for my, if I had to guess, worried-sick husband.

I didn't have my cell, and there were no working phone booths on the Tower property. All the fancy, red call boxes were for show and there wasn't a telephone inside. My next mistake was walking out of the security of the castle walls. I'd waited near the entrance of the Tower for nearly an hour thinking maybe Ghost would come out and find me. When he didn't, I went in search of a telephone. Finding none, I walked to the coffee house across the street and asked if I could use their phone, but once I explained it was a US number they said no. I even offered them a hundred pounds for their trouble—I was dismissed with a shake of the head.

Standing on the street corner at a complete loss, a taxi pulled up and stopped in the loading area. Then my next, very bad idea struck. If I could get back to the hotel, I could call Ghost and tell him where I was. Sure, he'd be over-the-top pissed but once he found out I was safe, he'd be relieved.

I approached the taxi and peered through the open window.

"Excuse me, sir, are you available?"

The man looked up from the newspaper he was reading and folded it in half before tossing it on the seat next to him.

"For a fit bird I am. Where to?"

Ignoring his comment may've been a mistake, too, but I was desperate to get back to the hotel. "The Park Plaza."

"No problem. Get in."

Relieved, I climbed in the cab, and away we went. One step closer to calling Ghost.

When the cab didn't immediately go over the Tower Bridge, I thought the driver knew a faster route, but after twenty minutes had passed and I saw a sign for the Swedenborg Gardens, I knew we were headed in the wrong direction.

"The Park Plaza," I reminded the driver.

"Yeah, yeah, I know."

"You must not because we're going in the wrong direction. I'm not paying you for a tour of the city. Please take me back."

"This is a shortcut," he lied, and my heart rate spiked.

Thirty minutes later, when he turned down a side street taking us away from the safety of the busy, traffic congested area, I understood why Ghost had made such a big deal about our taxi driver the first time we'd been in London. At the time, I'd stupidly thought Ghost had been overreacting by taking a picture of the driver's ID and threatening him with the police. Why hadn't I thought to do that before I got in? Somehow, I didn't think it'd have the same impact as it did when Ghost did it. God, I wished he was there.

The businesses and landmarks turned into a residential neighborhood. I watched in horror as houses gave way to an industrial area—I was fucked. I had to make a decision and fast.

"Please take me back to the Tower. I'll find another taxi."

"What, so you can stiff me? I told you I know where I'm going," the man angrily snipped.

The taxi started to slow for a stop sign, and I made my move. As soon as he came to a halt, I opened the door and I got out. My purse caught on the seat belt, and as I was fighting to get it free, the driver stepped on the gas and pulled away, leaving me no choice but jump out of the way and abandon my purse. The door slammed shut from the acceleration, and I watched in horror as my only hope to get back to Ghost sped away.

No money and no phone. I was royally fucked.

Ghost

"Rayne's missing," I said by way of greeting.

"Come again?"

"Rayne. She's missing. We were at the Tower of London and got separated. I can't find her."

"Fuck. How long?" Tex asked.

"A little over four hours."

"Four hours!"

My guts twisted hearing Tex repeat back how long it had been since I'd seen Rayne.

"I thought I'd find her wandering around looking for me. Either we're walking in circles, missing each other or . . ."

"Don't go there. I'll track her phone."

"You can't, it's at the hotel."

"No problem. Lucky for you, London has CCTV cameras everywhere. I'll have a lock on her in less than thirty minutes. Let me work, I'll call you back."

"Thirty minutes, Tex, then I'm tearing this city apart."

"First thing tomorrow I'm mailing a package to your house. I still don't know why you guys haven't outfitted your women with tracking devices. Makes my job a whole lot easier when you lose them."

"I don't plan on making a habit of losing my wife," I growled.

"Stand by." Tex hung up, and I began to pace.

Why did I leave the shop? That's right, to help a lost little girl. I was no better than the parents I'd thought badly of. Just because Rayne wasn't a child didn't mean she wasn't the most precious thing in my life.

Time seemed to stand still, each minute feeling like an hour. When Tex finally called back, I was ready to crawl out of my skin.

"She got into a taxi," he told me.

"A taxi? Was she alone?"

My heart pounded double-time in my chest. This was it; she'd been fucking taken. I knew it. In my stupidity I hadn't done the one thing I promised I'd do, protect her.

"Yes."

Fuck!

"Wait, what? She was alone?"

"Affirmative. She left the Tower gate and waited outside, near the ticket booth before she crossed the street and went into a Starbucks. She was in there a few minutes, came out empty handed, and stood on the corner. A taxi pulled up and she approached and got in."

"How long ago?"

"Almost an hour ago."

"Can you track the taxi?"

Hope bloomed in my chest. If Tex could find the taxi, I'd find Rayne.

"The taxi was caught by a traffic cam in front of Swedenborg Gardens almost thirty minutes ago."

"Swedenborg Gardens?"

Why the fuck would she be going there? We'd discussed going tomorrow, but she'd decided she'd rather see another palace. Had she changed her mind? Nothing was making sense. Rayne wouldn't leave and go off by herself. No fucking way.

"Yes. The taxi pulled off the main highway into a residential area. There are fewer cameras on those streets. It's going to take me a few minutes to try to pick up the taxi's location."

"Goddamn it!" I shouted, ignoring the people all around.

"We're going to find her. Hold tight."

"I can't hold tight. My pregnant wife is God knows where, alone, with no line of communication. I lost my ability to hold fucking tight four hours ago."

"Pregnant?"

"Yes," I spit out, not caring that we'd decided not to tell our friends until we could all get together for a barbecue. Keeping the secret seemed meaningless now. I needed Tex to understand the gravity of the situation.

As hard as it was, Tex was right, I had to calm down and think, but for the life of me I couldn't stop picturing Rayne afraid or hurt. I wiped my free hand over my face and took a deep breath.

Think, asshole, think. Slow down.

"Can you make out a cab company and ID number?" I asked.

"Let me go back and see," Tex answered. "Yes. The Queen's Royal Taxi. Number 07301998."

"Let me know if you can pick the cab back up. I have to make another call."

"Copy that."

I disconnected and called Oliver.

"Miss me already, mate?" His cheerful voice came over the line.

"I need your help."

"Anything." He quickly sobered, obviously hearing the desperation in my voice.

13

Rayne

My luck had gone from bad to worse.

I was now completely lost in the middle of nowhere. My travel guide and map were in my purse, which, of course, was in the back of the runaway taxi, along with my identification and credit cards. Thank God, my passport was at the hotel, locked in the safe, or I'd be stuck there. Blocks and blocks of factories with tall chain-link fences surrounding the buildings. I screamed for help, hoping someone would hear me, but to no avail. The buildings were too far from the road.

I wanted Ghost. I wanted to go home. I wanted to be cuddled up next to him in our bed, relaxing. Maybe traveling overseas was no longer in the cards for me. And my stomach was screaming at me for food. I wished I'd had more than a pastry for breakfast. Ghost had complained I wasn't eating enough, however morning sickness seemed to be setting in and the thought of more than a small croissant had made me want to hurl. Thankfully, it wasn't raining yet. The sky had started to cloud over, and I was waiting to be dumped on at any moment.

I looked around, trying to find any landmark in the skyline, but there was nothing. I couldn't even see the London Eye from where I was. I was completely turned around and all I knew was the sun was no longer directly overhead and had started to fall to the west. Not even that little piece of information helped me because I didn't know what damn direction the hotel was in. I wished Ghost were there. He could've steered us back to the hotel using his super-supreme navigational skills.

Oh my god, Ghost!

He had to be out of his mind; it'd been hours. Was he still wandering around the Tower trying to pick me out of the crowd?

A black town car drove by, and I wondered how dangerous hitchhiking in London was. It was the first car I'd seen in over a half hour. As the car passed by, I thought better of it. With my luck, the driver would be scarier than the cabbie. No way was I flagging down a car. Ghost was already going to kill me. I'd known better than to leave the security of the shop. Not only was I a seasoned traveler, but Ghost and Chase had preached about personal safety and situational awareness over the years—neither of which I used. The barrette Chase had given me and had saved my life back in Egypt wouldn't be any use now...not that I was even wearing it. I had no excuse, but self-recrimination wouldn't help me find a phone. There would be plenty of time for that later.

I had very few options at that point, none were good, but they were all I had. Find my way back to the main road and locate a business, or wait until the workday ended and people started exiting the gates. The cabbie had also driven through a residential area; maybe I could knock on doors until someone opened and let me use their phone.

Setting out in a new direction, I was determined to find help—and Ghost.

I rounded a corner and wanted to scream in frustration, industrial buildings as far as the eye could see. I stood on the corner, debating turning back, trying to retrace my steps for the third time when the town car slowly passed again, rolling to a stop not too far from me. A man stepped from the driver's side door and called out to me.

Shit. What would Ghost tell me to do? What would Chase say? Run! Never get into a car with a stranger. That was exactly what they'd tell me.

I turned and at the risk of looking like a crazy

woman, I started to jog away from the car. I only made it halfway down the block when the car turned around and followed me.

Panic started to set in, and I looked for someplace to hide. I flashed back to Egypt and the dirty mattress I'd been tied to. My wrists started to itch at the memory and sweat beaded on my forehead and ran down my face. I could taste the saltiness as I licked my now dry lips. Or were those tears? Between the lack of food, water, and my racing heart, my head started to swim. I couldn't let the man catch me. I wouldn't survive being hurt. Ghost would never recover. I had to keep running.

"Ma'am!" the man yelled again.

Shit. I needed to pick up my pace. My vision started to blur, and I couldn't go any faster. I tried to push on, but my legs were too heavy. I was light-headed and scared I'd fall and hurt the baby. I slowed to a stop and held onto a newspaper dispenser trying to catch my breath.

"Ma'am!" The man's voice was too close.

This was it. I was screwed. I couldn't do anything but scream, hoping someone would hear me and help.

I'm so sorry, Ghost!

Ghost

"Where's my wife, motherfucker?" I banged my fist on the worn, metal table and leaned in closer to the man who was the last person to see Rayne.

"I don't bloody know," he told me.

Oliver was standing next to me, his arms crossed over his wide chest and he, too, eyed the taxi driver. It'd taken him one call to the cab company to have the driver called back to the office. By the time Oliver had picked me up at the Tower of London, and we'd driven to the garage where the taxi service was housed, the driver had been waiting—unaware the wrath of Satan was about to rain down on him.

"Does this belong to your wife?" the manager asked, entering the break room.

Rayne's new leather purse dangled from his outstretched hand.

"Son of a bitch," I cursed.

Before I could move, Oliver had the driver out of the chair and pinned to the wall by his throat. Gone was the high-class gentleman he'd been the other night, and back was the lethal soldier I knew him to be.

"I think you may want to rethink your last statement and start talking. You have sixty seconds to tell my friend where his wife is. After that, I'm walking out the door and leaving him alone with you. I guarantee he will not be civil."

Oliver released some of the pressure from around the driver's throat, allowing him much needed oxygen.

The man sputtered and coughed before he started to speak again.

"A woman left that in my cab. I was going to place it into lost property."

Oliver stepped away, and I looked to the manager, who was shaking his head.

"It was in his locker," the manager informed me.

"For safe—"

"Shut the fuck up. Where is she?"

I took Rayne's purse from the manager and rummaged through the bag. Her wallet and credit cards were still in place, no cash, but I didn't think she had any, and if this fuckwit had stolen it that was the least of my concerns. Sunglasses, bottle of water, travel guide, and miscellaneous crap—nothing that would lead me to her.

Fuck! If I had her purse, that meant she didn't have her credit cards or identification.

I set the bag on the table and the strap caught my attention, it was scuffed. Further inspection showed the stitching of the strap was coming loose. I briefly closed my eyes and remembered the street artesian explaining he'd hand sewn all the bags. All his items were quality pieces; it would take quite a struggle to rip the stitching.

"Out we go." Oliver turned to the manager and ushered him to the door.

"If you're alive after he's done with you, you're fired. This is the third complaint filed against you."

"Third?" I asked.

"Yes. Harassment and theft. I didn't want to believe it. He is my wife's cousin. But after this—no more chances."

Seeing red didn't begin to describe what I was feeling. I wanted to rip his head off with my bare hands.

With slow, methodical steps, I made my way around the table.

"Did you touch her?" I growled, my voice no longer sounding like my own.

"No. No." The man held his hands in front of him as if the gesture could stop the imminent attack.

"Why do you have her purse?"

"I told you, she left it in my cab."

"You must think I'm a fucking idiot."

"She did. She left it."

It was time I schooled the asshole on how a Delta Force Operator extracts intel from an enemy combatant.

With a kick he didn't see coming, my foot perfectly connected with his solar plexus and he tumbled back, hitting the wall. Before he could catch his breath, two punches landed in the same spot, rendering him unable to speak. The man slid down the wall, landing on his ass, his body slumped forward as he gasped for air.

"Get up!" I yelled. When the man made no move to comply, I grabbed the collar of his button-down shirt and yanked him to his feet.

"Where is Rayne?" He took too long to answer, so I elbowed him across the face, happy to hear the crush of bones breaking before bringing it back across, hitting him a second time. A move the team affectionately called the stinger. Satisfied now that blood was pouring from his nose, dripping on his expensive and perfectly tailored shirt. I tried again. "Where did you take her?" The man mumbled something unintelligible. "Louder. What did you say?"

"Stop. Please stop. She got out over by White Hall."

"Got out?"

"I stopped at a stop sign, and she just jumped out. She was struggling with her bag, and I thought she was going to stiff me so I drove away." He coughed and used the back of his hand to wipe the blood from his mouth. "She just got out. That's all."

White Hall was in the opposite direction of the hotel, but it did correspond with the information Tex had given me about the taxi passing Swedenborg Gardens.

"Where did she ask to be taken when she got in?"

"Park Plaza."

My blood pressure kicked up another notch. This asshole had pegged Rayne as an easy mark and had intended to take her around the city to hike up his meter.

"Where exactly did she get out?"

"Blue Bonnet and Royal Walk."

Having all the information I needed from him, I balled my fist and felt no remorse when a sharp uppercut to his chin knocked him clean out. He crumbled to the floor, and I used the remaining control I had not to spit on him as I stepped over his beaten body.

The door swung open, and Oliver stepped in.

"Bloody hell, I was afraid you were going to kill him." Oliver looked down at the man. "You didn't, right? A dead body will take me more than a call to fix."

"His nose is broken, and I think I saw a tooth fly out of his mouth, but he'll wake up."

"I heard. Blue Bonnet and Royal Walk. Let's go."

Oliver didn't wait for me to respond, just like in Afghanistan, he trusted I'd pull up his six.

Hold on, Princess, I'm coming for you.

14

Meghan

"Where would you like to take her, ma'am?" Tomas, my personal security officer and driver asked.

"I don't know," I answered before looking back at the woman lying across the back seat. "Rayne? Wake up."

Where was Ghost? Why was she out here all alone? I looked out the tinted windows, scanning the area, expecting to see her frantic husband searching for her.

"I'm afraid I gave her a fright. Should we take her to hospital?"

Crap. She was pregnant and passed out cold. This was not good. I couldn't think of any reason Rayne would be wandering around this part of the city.

"I have to call Harry," I announced. Yes, he would know what to do and he could get in touch with Ghost.

"Ma'am, he's in meetings all afternoon," Tomas reminded me.

I was about to relent and agree to take Rayne to the hospital when I remembered the stories Harry had told me about Afghanistan and Ghost and his team saving his life. They were close, he spoke of Ghost fondly. He'd want to be interrupted.

I pulled my phone from my bag at my feet and dialed, hoping I was doing the right thing. Harry knew I'd never call when he was busy unless it was an emergency.

"Meghan? Are you all right?" he answered, just as I knew he would.

"Yes," I reassured him. "I was coming back from lunch in White Hall and I saw Rayne walking down the street. I asked Tomas to pull over so I could say hello and I think we scared her. She took off running. Harry, she passed out. What do I do?"

"Where's Ghost?"

"I don't know. She doesn't have a phone or a purse. Did you miss the part where I told you she was passed out?"

"Ghost isn't with her?"

"No," I huffed, getting more worried by the second.

"Bring her to the palace. I'll try to get ahold of Ghost." I heard him excusing himself from the meeting and felt horrible for all the trouble I'd caused.

"I'm sorry for bothering you."

"You are never a bother, my love. You did the right thing. If she's lost, I fear what Ghost will do to my poor city trying to find her. Bring her to the palace, hurry."

"Harry?"

"Right here."

"Which palace?"

He chuckled, and I rolled my eyes. I was learning, but sometimes he forgot I wasn't fluent in royalty yet.

"Buckingham."

"Please find Ghost and tell him I'm sorry."

Harry

Bloody hell.

Ghost wasn't answering his phone.

I hated to bother Oliver on his day off, but no one was better at tracking than him. Just like me, he would do anything for the man who'd not only saved our lives but kept our secrets. Yes, Oliver would want to help.

When he didn't answer as well, I left him an urgent message to ring me back.

The only thing I could do for my friend was keep his wife protected until he could come fetch her. That meant medical care as well. After making arrangements for my personal physician to come to the palace, all that was left to do was wait.

Rayne

"She'll be fine. Dehydration and exhaustion. Nothing a little rest won't fix."

"Are you sure? One hundred percent? Does she need the hospital? She's with child."

I could hear voices around me, but my eyelids were too heavy to open.

"Your Royal Highness, she's being properly cared for here."

Royal Highness? That woke me up in a hurry. My eyes flew open, and I tried to sit up.

"Whoa, Rayne. You're okay. Lie still." A deep voice tried to reassure me.

"What?"

"Thank God, you're awake," a female voice said from beside me.

"Meghan?"

"Yes, Rayne, it's me."

"What happened? Where am I?"

"I'm afraid I scared you half to death, and you passed out. I'm so sorry."

"Passed out?" I tried to think about the last thing I remembered. The black car, running, trying to catch my breath.

"That was you? In the town car?"

"Yes. I'm sorry."

"Thank God." I relaxed, then I remembered why I was in the industrial park in the first place. "Ghost!" I sat up, not caring the prince had asked me not to move. He could've been the King of . . . well, England, and I wouldn't have cared. "I need to find Ghost. Now. Right now."

"Slow down," Harry soothed. "I've placed a call to him. Tell us what happened."

After explaining everything from the beginning, not leaving anything out, Harry cursed, and whether it was from relief at being safe or shock such a sophisticated man could utter such profanity, I fell back on the bed and laughed.

"Are you sure she's okay? I think she's gone mad. Why is she laughing?" Harry asked.

His concern made me laugh harder until Meghan joined in the hilarity.

"Harry, I think she's laughing at you. I hardly think she was expecting you to say fuck."

"And why the bloody hell not? This is a clusterfuck, as Ghost would say. He has to be out of his mind. And why the hell is no one calling me back?"

I stopped laughing when he reminded me how worried Ghost had to have been.

"Please help me find him," I begged.

"Tomas, please contact Chief Young. I want every resource used to find Keane Bryson within the hour.

After you make the call, take Lucas and go look for him."

"Yes, Your Royal Highness."

"I'm so sorry to put you through so much trouble."

"No trouble," he told me.

"Where am I?" I finally looked around the room, soft yellow walls and a four-poster bed, complete with a canopy. The large windows were covered in draperies, the fabric complemented the soft, soothing tones of the room. A salmon colored love seat sat in front of a magnificent fireplace. And, finally, the largest mirror I'd ever seen majestically hung above the mantelpiece.

"Buckingham Palace," Meghan answered.

"What?" I was back to sitting. "I'm not allowed to be in here."

"You are allowed to be wherever I see fit. Meghan and I are going to step out so you can speak to Dr. Stanly in private. He says you're fine, however I'd like him to check you once more now that you are awake."

"Wait." Harry stopped and looked over his shoulder. "Please don't be offended, but I don't know how to properly address you now that we're not in private."

"Sir will suffice since we are in the palace." He looked almost embarrassed. "Meghan is to be addressed as ma'am."

"Thank you, sir, for all your kindness."

He started for the door when Meghan leaned close and whispered. "I'm sorry."

"For what?"

"For all the formality. I'm still just Meghan—your friend."

"Actually, you're my super-secret-duchess friend." I laughed. "Thank you for saving me."

"Right place, right time. I'm glad you're okay."

She followed Harry and quietly clicked the door closed behind her.

I hoped someone found Ghost soon. Now that I was safe, I was even more worried about his state of mind.

Ghost

It was dark. Fucking dark, and Rayne was somewhere walking the streets. I was getting ready to come unglued. No, that wasn't true, I'd lost my sanity hours ago. Tex still hadn't picked Rayne up on any of the CCTV cameras around London, and Oliver and I had started at the intersection the cabbie had given us and worked our way out and still hadn't found her.

Oliver's phone shrilled, breaking the silence of the car.

"Your Royal Highness. Now is not a good— What?" The car came to a screeching halt and Oliver made a very illegal U-turn down a one-way street and accelerated at a speed that had me pinned to my seat.

"What the fuck?" I barked.

"Yes. We'll be right there." Oliver disconnected and tossed his phone in the cupholder.

"What is it?"

"Harry has Rayne."

"Where? Is she okay? How did he find her?"

"Buckingham Palace. His physician has seen her, she's fine. And I don't know."

"Physician?"

"That was all he said. She's worried sick about you and wants you now."

"She's worried about *me*?"

"Hold on, mate, this is going to be like the good old days, minus the Taliban shooting at us."

"Why the fuck didn't he call us?" I asked, pulling my phone out of my pocket. "Shit, mine's dead."

"I'm afraid there is no service in most of the old buildings. And I didn't exactly want to waste time checking my voicemail when we left. My fault, Mate."

"Nothing's your fault, Oliver. Thank you for all your help."

"Don't mention it."

I would've been nervous with the way Oliver was driving if I hadn't been so eager to get to Rayne. Red lights were ignored, he drove on the wrong side of the road, and even used the bike lane to get around traffic.

We were in a high-speed chase without the chase. I white-knuckled the oh-shit bar to my left and fought the urge to close my eyes as he continued to weave through traffic. With each revolution of his tires he brought me that much closer to my wife.

He barely slowed as he approached the back entrance of the palace, the large, golden gates were open and ready for our arrival. He pulled around, coming to a stop under a large, stone archway. The prince appeared in the open doorway, worry etched in his face.

I pushed the car door open and bolted across the tarmac toward Spike. Oliver didn't bother turning the car off when he, too, jumped out and jogged the short distance.

"She's safe and resting upstairs," Spike said immediately, trying to placate me. "I'll take you to her."

He led us through a staff kitchen to a set of stairs, taking two at a time until we came to a landing with a closed door that read: First Floor Gallery. Before he opened the door, he turned to me.

"She's very worried you're upset with her."

"Upset? I've been scared to fucking death all day. My heart feels like it's been ripped from my chest."

"I'll let her explain what happened. But I want to warn you, she has an IV. Just to rehydrate her. I insisted it stay in until you got here even though she complained she felt fine."

I closed my eyes and wasn't sure if I wanted to weep with joy or go back to the room with the taxi driver and beat the hell out of him some more.

"Thank you," I choked out. "I owe you my life."

"You don't owe me anything. What are mates for if not to watch out for one another?"

"Thank you all the same."

"It's my pleasure. Come, I'll take you to your sleeping beauty."

He opened the door leading to a grand lobby, and I tried my best to stand tall and look respectable. I wasn't sure if I was pulling it off or not, and if I had to guess it would be a negative. All I wanted was to see Rayne.

Spike opened the door, and there she was sleeping in the middle of a huge canopy bed, looking every bit of the princess I knew she was.

I stepped into the room and willed my legs not to buckle. I noted Meghan was sitting vigil by Rayne's bedside and would have to thank her later. All I wanted to do was pull my wife into my arms and breathe her in.

Meghan stood and smiled, and with a nod of acknowledgment she moved to leave. I kicked my shoes off and climbed into bed next to Rayne. The door shut, and I scooted as close to her as I could. Her eyes came open and after a moment, they widened before she tried to sit up.

"Relax, Princess."

"Ghost! You're here. I'm sorry. I'm so, so—"

"Shhh. Everything's fine now." I swallowed the lump in my throat before I continued. "I missed you."

"I missed you, too. I was so worried." She began to cry.

"So was I." I gathered her in my arms and let her sob. Her body shook within my embrace, and I'd never been so thankful to hold her. Relief washed over me and the adrenaline crash hit me like a ton of bricks. I was bone tired and all I wanted now was to sleep for a week with Rayne safely tucked next to me.

15

Rayne

I was startled awake when the bed dipped, and I was rolled to my side. I opened my eyes to find Ghost staring at me.

"Morning, Princess."

"Morning."

The smell of bacon drifted around the room, and my stomach came alive.

"Hungry?" Ghost chuckled when my tummy grumbled.

"Yes. Starving."

"Good. Spike sent up a full spread."

The prince. Meghan. The palace. How could I have forgotten?

"Ghost!"

"Right here, Princess."

I couldn't stop the matching smile that formed upon seeing Ghost so happy. The relief I felt was profound. All was well as long as he was by my side.

"I'm so sorry about yesterday. I can't believe I was so stupid and left the store."

"None of it was your fault. It was mine. I never should've let you out of my sight. I'm the one who's sorry."

"But I knew better than to leave."

"Let's talk about this over breakfast, and you're eating a big meal this morning. Doctor's orders. Spike and Meghan are here; would you mind if they joined us? He thought you'd feel more comfortable eating up here."

"They're still here? Yes. Of course."

"You go clean up, and I'll let them know we're ready."

"Are you saying I look a mess?" I was sure I did, but I couldn't help teasing Ghost.

"A beautiful mess. Please hurry, I really want you to eat something. You only had one pastry yesterday. You and the baby need food."

"Speaking of, I have a surprise for you."

"You want to have palace sex?"

"No." I playfully shoved his chest. But now that he'd mentioned it, palace sex did sound fun. But Ghost was right. I needed to eat, and we needed to talk. As happy as I was to be in his arms, I still had an uneasy feeling. I was afraid once he heard about my series of dumb decisions he'd be pissed.

"What's wrong?" He cradled my face and brushed his thumb across my cheek. "Why do you look so upset?"

"I'm afraid you're going to be mad at me."

"Princess, all I care about is that you're safe and sound and in my arms. I was scared shitless yesterday, worst six hours and forty-three minutes of my life. I had no idea where you were, if you were hurt, hungry, scared. Fuck, I let you down. All I kept thinking about was how it was my fault you were out in the city alone, not even a week into our marriage and I'd already broken my promise to you."

"You didn't let me down. You found me."

"I didn't find you, Meghan did. I was getting close but—" My stomach growled loudly, and Ghost stopped mid-sentence. "Up you go. We'll talk about the rest over breakfast."

"So bossy."

I got out of bed and when my bare feet hit the plush carpet, I understood the meaning of luxury. It felt like I was walking on pillow soft clouds. The en suite was a tad overdone for my taste: gold trimmed the ceiling and bathroom fixtures, more centuries-old artwork hung on the walls, and marble floors, which were surprisingly warm. The only part of the room I did like was the huge, claw-foot tub. I could picture

Ghost and me relaxing in a warm bath with candle light dancing on all the shiny surfaces.

Finding a note from Meghan with my name on it sitting on top of a bag of toiletries, I gratefully tore open the toothbrush and quickly brushed my teeth and combed my hair, pulling it into a ponytail. By the time I was done, Meghan and Harry were already seated on the love seat, and an impressive spread of breakfast dishes was displayed on a white-linen-covered table.

"Good morning, Rayne." The prince stood and greeted me. "Glad you have some color back this morning."

"Good morning, sir. Thank you again for all your help yesterday and for allowing me to stay the night."

"No trouble."

"Ma'am." I turned to Meghan and smiled when she rolled her eyes. I wondered what Mary and the other girls would think of her. I had to suppress a laugh when I thought about what Meghan would think of Mary. She was an acquired taste; her larger than life and straight-forward personality were a lot to take in. But once she let you in and allowed you to see the real her, there was no one more loyal or protective. You couldn't find a better friend than Mary Laughlin.

Ghost waited for me to sit in a high-backed wing chair before he took his own seat.

"You must be starving after your great adventure

yesterday. Help yourself," Meghan offered, pointing to all the yummy food.

I didn't want to be rude, but I *was* hungry. I piled my plate with eggs and bacon, wondering if I could fit a Danish on the fine china without looking like an uncivilized pig. Deciding I didn't care, I grabbed one and sat back to dig in.

Light conversation carried on around me, but I was too focused on my food to pay attention. The mention of Oliver's name drew me away from the cheese-filled pastry, and my ears perked up. I didn't remember seeing Oliver yesterday.

"Oliver was with you?" I asked Ghost.

"Yes. Once Tex found you getting in a taxi on the CCTV, I called Oliver."

"Tex? You called Tex?"

"Yes, he sends his congratulations and he's sending me a tracking device. You're to wear it at all times. You'll have three choices, a watch, a pair of earrings, and a necklace. But anytime you leave the house you need to wear one of them."

Maybe I should've balked at the directive; he was *telling* me I was going to wear a tracking device. Not a moment's consideration was given to if I minded, effectively, being low-jacked. However, oddly, I felt cherished. A beautiful warmth washed over me knowing what lengths Ghost would go to to keep me safe.

"Okay."

"Start from the beginning, what happened?" Meghan asked.

Ghost's face turned to stone, and I reached across the small distance and placed my hand over his forearm and squeezed. His face relaxed a fraction, then he began recounting our day at the Tower of London.

He stopped, and on a sharp inhale he continued, "There was this little girl, she, literally, ran right into me. She was lost, and the bit— excuse me, the woman behind the counter wouldn't call for a security officer to come to the store, instead she told me to take her to their office next door. That was my mistake. I left the gift shop, leaving Rayne unprotected."

"Was she okay? Did you find her parents?" I gasped. "The poor thing must've been terrified. Someone could've taken her."

"Yes. Her parents were already in the security office reporting her missing."

"Thank God, she ran into you and not some sleaze-ball pedophile. I bet her parents were grateful. My husband, the superhero swooping in to save lost little girls." I smiled, proud that he'd helped reunite the family.

I know how freaked out Emily gets when Annie takes off on her tank cruising around the property on an imaginary combat mission and she loses sight of her. And they have more cameras surrounding their house than the Pentagon. Emily would lose her shit if Annie got lost at some place like the Tower of London.

"You know what I was thinking when the girl spilled her drink on me? I was annoyed. And when she couldn't find her parents I was pissed, wondering what kind of idiots lose their child." Shame marred his handsome face, and he shook his head. "I'm such an asshole. I was going to lambast the parents for inconveniencing me and explain all the things that could've happened to their child in their absence. But when the mother turned around and fell to her knees in relief, I realized she already knew and was terrified. Then when I went back to the shop and you were gone—I'd lost you, the most precious and important thing in my life—I understood."

"What did you understand?"

"The fear of not knowing. The terror."

"I'm sorry I left the shop. I thought maybe you'd gone outside to get away from the crowd. I knew better but . . . I was stupid."

"Where did you go?"

I explained walking around looking for him, leaving the fortress, going to the Starbucks to try find a phone to call him, getting in the cab, and finally wandering around the neighborhood.

"And when the town car pulled over, I thought I was about to get abducted." I laughed.

Ghost found nothing funny about my imagined-kidnapping. Neither did Meghan.

"Oh my God! I'm so sorry." She covered her mouth with both hands. "I just wanted to say hi."

"Are you kidding? I'd been walking around for hours and was so turned around I was going in circles. It was a miracle you showed up when you did."

I hated to think how many more hours I would've been walking around if Meghan hadn't found me when she did.

"I heard you bloodied up the cabbie well and good," Harry announced and smiled.

"What?"

Ghost

Damn.

I really wished Spike hadn't told Rayne there'd been a fight. She was well versed when it came to my job, but I still didn't like her hearing about the violence.

"He'll be fine."

"Sure, after his nose is reset and some dental surgery." He continued to laugh.

"Are you okay?" Rayne turned to me, her soft hand on my bare skin calming my rioting nerves. I just wanted to forget yesterday happened. The more I thought about what could've happened to her, the higher my blood pressure spiked. I could've lost her forever. The what-ifs were unbearable. What if the taxi driver had tried to touch her instead of just wanting to jack up the meter and rip her off? What if Meghan hadn't found her when she did and Rayne was left passed out on the sidewalk? Fuck. The possibilities were endless.

Rayne's hand tightened on my arm, and I fought the images, coming back to the present.

"Yes, Princess. I'm fine." Wanting to change the subject I added, "I thought you had a surprise for me?"

"Oh, yeah!" Her beautiful face came alive, and joy took over her whole being. That was what I liked to see. My wife smiling and happy. There was no place for worry and concern in her life, not when it came to me. "Yesterday when the doctor came to see me, he checked the baby's heartbeat. Since you weren't here, and I didn't have my phone, Her Royal Highness was nice enough to record it for us."

"Yes. Yes. Yes. I have it. Here." Meghan pulled her phone out of her handbag. Sliding her finger across the screen she brought up an app before handing it to me. "Just press play."

A rustling sound filled the room, then a steady swooshing beat.

Holy shit. I was going to be a dad. The audible confirmation made it more real. There was a baby growing inside of Rayne. My baby. *Our* baby. We'd created a life. She and I blended together to make one tiny, perfect human.

"That's it? That's his heartbeat?" I choked out, willing myself to keep my emotions in check.

"His or hers, yes."

"Everything's okay. The baby's healthy?"

"The baby is perfect. One hundred and sixty beats per minute. Exactly what it's supposed to be."

"Will you send the recording to me?" I asked Meghan, forcing myself to hand her back the device that held my child's first sign of life.

"Already done. Harry did it last night." She beamed. "We were hoping you'd be too busy with Rayne to check your email and ruin her surprise."

Rayne's cheeks flushed at Meghan's innuendo.

"Did you get enough to eat?" I asked. Not wanting to be rude to our hosts but eager to get Rayne alone.

"Yes. I'm stuffed." Rayne placed her plate on the table and sat back in the chair, placing both hands on her stomach. "Everything was delicious."

"I had some clothes brought in for you," Meghan started. "Nothing fancy, but I figured you'd like to change before heading out."

"Oh my God, yes. That was really nice of you."

Meghan and Rayne both stood and walked to the bed to inspect the shopping bags, giving me a moment alone with Spike.

"I can't ever repay you for—"

"I already told you there's nothing to repay. Get yourselves cleaned up. Meghan and I have our own surprise for Rayne."

"Anything you say, Your Royal Highness," I joked.

"Aren't you a cheeky bastard this morning? Go fetch your wife and meet us outside when you're done." He stood and offered his hand, which I gladly accepted. "And don't take too long." He winked.

I hated to disappoint, but I had a feeling we'd be late for whatever surprise Spike had arranged. There was a very large shower calling my name, and I planned on using it for however long it took for Rayne to be thoroughly satisfied.

16

Ghost

"Ghost. I can't," Rayne panted.

"Yes, you can. Again, Princess. Come on my cock one more time."

I had Rayne bent over in the shower and was debating remodeling our bathroom when we got home. The large space allowed me take her at the perfect angle. Her hands braced on the wall, legs spread, and her back beautifully arched. Her tattoo was on display, but that wasn't what held my attention today. I watched as my cock tunneled in and out of her pussy. Each time I pulled out, it glistened with her excitement. Her first orgasm was fast and explosive, taking the edge off enough for me to work her back up and tease her until we could both fall over the cliff into bliss together.

"Ghost," she whined. Reaching my hand around, I found her clit and started to rub in slow, firm circles. "More."

Her hips bucked in sync with my thrusts, and her inner muscles started to tighten.

"That's it, Rayne. Let go," I coaxed, needing her to hurry. "I'm almost there," I grunted and adjusted my pace.

A tingling had started at the base of my spine, and my balls drew up in preparation for my fast approaching orgasm. Her pussy clamped down around my cock, and her legs shook as her orgasm broke.

"Holy Christ," I growled and couldn't hold back the rush of euphoria. I pulled out of the warmth of her body and jerked my cock, fighting to keep my eyes open to watch as my come marked her firm ass and back. When my orgasm finally stopped, I rubbed the evidence over her tattoo. It was barbaric and probably made me seem like a Neanderthal, but I couldn't give the first fuck. I needed the reminder she was mine and I was hers. Nothing would ever take her from me.

I helped Rayne stand and pulled her into my arms.

"Palace shower sex." She giggled.

"I love you so fucking much."

I didn't let her return the sentiment. I needed to taste her pretty lips. Needed to feel her tongue dance with mine. But more than anything I needed the connection, the confirmation our love could and would withstand anything.

Rayne

"Are you serious?" I asked, unable to hide my shock and excitement.

My heart was thundering in my chest. There was no way Harry was suggesting what I thought he was.

"You told me your favorite part of your first trip to London with Ghost was seeing the balcony," Meghan reminded me. "I remember when I was a kid and visited London, I had my picture taken in front of this very same balcony. So since you're here and all . . ." She trailed off and gestured to the open French doors leading to the famous stone balcony.

"We can't. There are people down there. Won't you get in trouble?"

"Trouble?" The prince laughed. "Trouble's my middle name. Or it was until I met this shining beauty." Mischief laced his tone, but his eyes told a different story when he gazed adoringly at his wife.

"Go on. Give the crowd a show," Meghan urged.

"Let this be our wedding present to you," Harry added.

"Come on, Princess, let's go see this balcony you like so much."

"Like? It's where royal fairytales are sealed with a kiss. I don't just like it, I love it. It's every little girl's fantasy to meet her Prince Charming and live happily ever after."

"I'm no Prince Charming but I do promise you a happily ever after." Ghost tugged my hand, pulling me through the doorway onto the stone landing. I sucked in a breath at the enormity of my surroundings. He took another step, leading us closer to the railing that overlooked the courtyard below. The large, golden gates of the palace came into view, the Victoria Statue stood tall and proud beyond the confines of the palace. People were milling about, sightseeing and taking pictures. And I could see St. James Park in the distance.

Ghost took me in his arms and smiled down at me.

"Is it everything you dreamed it would be?"

I took in his face—open and happy. Yes, *he* was everything I'd hoped he would be. My Prince Charming. He didn't sweep me off my feet while galloping in on a white horse, instead he rescued me wearing all black, swooping in like an avenging hero in a romance novel. Our fairytale didn't start with a carriage and courtship; it began with a one-night stand and a C-130 military transport plane.

"No. I could've never dreamed up a man as perfect as you in a million years," I told him.

"To fairytales," Ghost murmured before he closed the distance and kissed me with a passion I was sure this balcony had never seen. It was far too indecent for royal protocol and more indicative of lust rather than love. However, when he slowed the kiss and swept me back, causing one foot to come off the ground for balance, I felt every bit the princess he called me.

Our lips parted, and I whispered, "To fairytales."

Ghost set me on my feet and made sure I was settled before stepping back. I knew we didn't have much time left and there was still something we had to do. "One question before we go in." I lowered my voice, making sure no one could hear me. "Where are we going to carve our names?"

"Such a rebel." Ghost feigned shock. "I know just the place." He tugged my hand and walked around one of the large stone pillars. He stopped and knelt down. To anyone looking it would seem he was tying his boot, however, with his penknife in hand, he quickly carved our mark into the centuries old railing.

P+G

"When did you become such a sap?" I laughed. "Not that I'm complaining."

Ghost stared at me for a long moment before looking over the railing, then back to me.

"The day this stunning spitfire barged into my life and showed me all the things I'd been missing. Her love and candor opened a world I never knew I could have. A place where fairytales exist, and a beautiful princess named Rayne—with a Y and an E—reigns supreme for all eternity."

I practically knocked him over when I lunged, wrapping my arms around his neck and burying my face in his chest. His strong heartbeat strummed under my cheek, reminding me all was right in my world. I was back where I belonged.

With Ghost.

EPILOGUE

Rayne

The last few days had been a whirlwind as we tried to pack in as much as possible before we left. The only hitch had been that any time we left the room, Ghost held my hand so tightly, his knuckles turned white. The first day I'd allowed it. We'd both needed the connection and reassurance the other was near. However, the second day, on the way to breakfast in the hotel lobby, he was even more on edge. His head was on a swivel, scanning the area like we were in a war zone.

I hated it.

I hated that Ghost was so stressed he wasn't enjoying what was left of our honeymoon. When I wrenched my hand out of his grasp, he looked as though I'd cut his heart from his chest. He didn't say anything, but I knew I had to put a stop to his worrying.

"I have my cell phone right here." I held it up to show him. "And I have a hundred pounds tucked in my bra," I whispered. "Everything's fine."

"But—"

"No buts, Ghost. I'm safe. You're right here. And even if you weren't, I'd still be fine. You can't drive yourself crazy like this."

"If something happens to you—"

"Nothing's going to happen to me."

He still hadn't looked convinced, but he was no longer holding my hand like I was his hostage.

Progress.

After one last dinner at Mickey's, we called it an early night and headed back to the hotel to pack and get ready for our flight in the morning. Ghost had been teasing me all day with soft kisses and inconspicuous touches. To the passersby, it wouldn't have looked to be more than an innocent display of affection, but that was only because they couldn't hear his whispered promises of sexual debauchery.

By the time we'd made it back to Park Plaza, I was ready to jump him in the fancy lobby. So, when the concierge stopped us to tell Ghost we'd had a package delivered to the hotel, I wanted to scream in protest.

"This will only take a second." He chuckled, knowing I was eager to get upstairs.

It was the last night of my honeymoon; I planned to enjoy every second of what was left and that included my husband and a bed.

With the box in hand, we made our way to the room. The door had barely shut behind us when Ghost set the unopened box on the dresser, stripped us of our clothes, and tossed me on the bed. His face went between my legs and he ate me like a man possessed. It took me less than five minutes to come in his mouth. The smug look on his face faded when I pushed him to his back, crawled on his lap, and sank onto his cock.

"That's it, Princess, harder," Ghost groaned and dug his fingers into my hips. "Grind down."

I used his chest to anchor myself and glided up and down, trying my hardest to get him to come first. Under normal circumstances it was useless; he had more willpower than any one person should have and always made sure I got off first. But today, I was on a mission. I wanted him to lose his iron control. It was starting to slip, but he was still holding strong. I had to up my efforts.

"Do you like what you see?"

I sat up and cupped both my breasts, pushing them together.

"Rayne," he warned.

"I think you do. Do you like watching me play with them, Ghost?"

His eyes widened when I pinched my nipples, and

his hands flexed. Sliding down his long shaft I kept him deep, not moving, just tightening my inner muscles.

"Holy fuck," he moaned and threw his head back on the pillow. Perfect, I almost had him.

I started to rock back and forth, staying upright, not taking my hands from my breasts.

"Lean down, I want your tits in my face."

"No way."

I knew what he wanted. If I leaned forward and rocked, my clit would rub against his pelvis, and I would lose the game. I was too close.

Ghost moved his hands from my waist up to my breasts and knocked my hands away, replacing them with his. His coarse, work-worn palms abraded my sensitive nipples, and my body jolted, pleasure and pain mingled as he pinched and pulled.

"Ghost," I said on a moan.

"That's it, sweetheart, lean forward so I can taste your nipples," he cajoled. I did as he asked, forgetting I wanted to make him come undone before me this time.

He flattened his tongue, licking one, then the other before latching on and sucking. With his hands now free and my breasts in his face like he wanted, he started rocking my hips. I braced my hands on either side of his head and gave up on winning. My orgasm was building too fast.

"Almost."

"That's it, Rayne, come on my cock, take me with you, Princess," he said, releasing one nipple before moving to the other side. His lips had barely touched my skin when the dam I'd been holding back broke, and my body locked. Ghost took over, thrusting up, prolonging my orgasm. When he finally pulled me down one last time and held me still, his cock twitched and pulsed inside of me, and he shouted his release.

"Rayne."

I relaxed in his arms and lowered myself until I was lying flat against his chest.

"I win," he said after he caught his breath. "But it was a nice try."

"What?" I tried to play coy.

"Princess, you always try, and while I love to watch you turn into my sexy temptress, I will always take care of you first."

"But I want—"

"No buts. You're always first."

I sighed and kissed his chest, appreciating the muscles under my lips.

"I love you, Ghost."

"I love you, too, Princess."

GHOST

"We never opened the box last night." Rayne reminded me. "Who's it from?"

We still had a few hours before we had to leave, and though we'd had sex on every available surface in the room, I wanted more. When Rayne stood and walked to the dresser, only my shirt covering her curves, my cock twitched in appreciation.

"I think it's from Harry and Meghan. It's addressed to Princess and Ghost."

"Open it," I urged, wanting her to hurry back to bed.

She opened the folded cardstock and read, "'Rayne, it was a pleasure to meet the lovely woman who captured Ghost's heart. May you have a long and happy marriage. Ghost, don't be a stranger, mate. We expect to see you again after you welcome your child. God help us all, a new generation of mini-Ghosts running around. On a side note, the twit from the Tower has been tossed on her arse. I'm deeply sorry for the trouble she caused.'"

She looked up from the note, her brows pulled together.

"He had her fired? It wasn't her fault."

"Yeah, Princess, it was. And not only that, she allowed a stranger to leave the store with a lost child. That shit was dangerous. Anything could've happened." I tried to tamp down the anger welling up.

"I guess you're right. There's more." She looked

back at the note and continued to read. "I'll send a car to pick you up. Wouldn't want you getting lost on the way to the airport or to have to beat up another cabbie. All the best, Spike Wells.'"

"Ass." I chuckled.

"That was nice of him." She set the note down and opened the box. "Holy shit. These are the gifts I left at the Tower shop. Even Annie's sword is in here."

Fucking Spike, leave it to him to think of the souvenirs. I'd been so wrapped up in Rayne, gifts had been the last thing on my mind.

"Are you ever going to tell me what really happened in Afghanistan?" she asked.

"You know what happened. Spike and Oliver told you." Part of the story at least. I was happy they'd left out most of what had happened. I didn't need Rayne worrying more than she already did when the team left on a mission.

"Somehow, I think they left out the good stuff."

"There was nothing good about Afghanistan," I told her.

"You know what I mean. The parts where my super-sexy, secret-Delta husband swoops in and saves the day."

"Sexy, huh?"

"Super-sexy." She winked.

"You should come back to bed and point out all the sexy parts you like."

"It would take too long."

"There's that many?" I asked, enjoying Rayne's playfulness.

"So many. From the top of your handsome head all the way down to your perfect toes."

"Any parts in particular that are your favorite?"

"Oh, yeah."

"I think you need to come over here and show me just those parts." She stepped toward the bed, her eyes eating up my bare chest as she came. "Lose the shirt, Rayne."

She pulled the shirt over her head and tossed it aside, giving me an unobstructed view of her delicious body.

"You are so fucking beautiful."

Her hands hit the foot of the bed, and she crept up. I looked over her back to the mirror behind her, her ass and pussy on full display. Once she'd crawled over my thighs, she stopped to pull the sheet down. My cock bobbed, ready for whatever she had in mind.

"This part right here is one of my favorites." She leaned forward, her nipples grazing my leg as she licked the pre-come weeping from the head.

I yanked another pillow from beside me and used it to prop myself further up. My eyes darted from the mirror to her mouth, trying to decide which view I liked better.

"Fuck, I love your mouth," I groaned when she put the head of my cock in her mouth and sucked.

She slowly worked my shaft in and out, taking only millimeters each time. Then she lowered her head until the tip was pressed to the back of her throat, and I thought I was going to come. I thought about it, giving into my desire like she wanted, but it felt too good; I wanted more. And more than that, I wanted her to come with me.

"Move your ass over here," I instructed.

With one last look in the mirror, I caught sight of her pussy and had to close my eyes before I lost control. She moved over until I could reach everything I wanted.

"You're gonna come with me, Princess." Her thighs quivered when I ran my hand from the back of her knee to the crease of her ass and stopped. "Spread your legs wider." She did as I said, and my fingers found her wet and ready. "Don't stop sucking me off. If your mouth stops, so do my fingers."

She hummed her approval, sending goose bumps racing over my arms. Goddamn, that felt good.

I pushed three fingers in her pussy and started slowly moving them in and out until she pushed back on my hand, wanting more. I pulled my fingers free, then plunged my ring and middle finger back in, leaving my index finger to play with her clit. She jolted at the contact, and her teeth scraped the base of my cock, adding a touch of pain. Her tongue followed, soothing the ache.

"I'm not going to come until you do. It's up to you how long we stay like this."

Her hand went to my balls, and her pace quickened, just as I knew it would. Rayne rose to the challenge and was all in, trying to make me come first.

"Grab them harder, Princess, roll them in your hand," I directed and thrusted my hips. "Fuck. Just like that. Are you ready to come?"

She shook her head the best she could with my cock in her throat and swallowed around the head. I was seeing stars when I intensified my efforts, adding more pressure to her clit and moving my fingers in a come here motion. I had nothing to worry about; she'd be coming in a matter of seconds.

"I can feel your pussy tightening around my fingers, Rayne. You're there, you can't stop it. Come on, Princess, come for me."

The fluttering deep inside her had turned to a steady pulsing until she couldn't hold back and shook and moaned her orgasm just in the nick of time. I threw my head back and closed my eyes, enjoying the pleasure Rayne was pulling from my body.

So damn good.

Rayne

The ride to Heathrow in the limo Harry and Meghan had sent for us was a much nicer way to get to the airport. Ghost had timed everything perfectly, so we'd arrived with just enough time to check in, go through security, and find our gate number on the large display in the common waiting area. There was only thirty minutes before we had to board the flight.

It was so much better than having to wait in a packed airport for hours. He found our seats in first class and got everything situated before sitting next to me and settling in.

"Ready to go home?" he asked.

"Yes, I miss everyone. But I'm sad to leave London."

"We'll be back," he reminded me.

"Yeah, we have a twenty-five year anniversary scavenger hunt to go on."

"I'm sure we'll be back before that."

I looked around the quickly filling plane and wondered if Lou Anne was on the flight but didn't see her.

"Everything okay?"

"Of course. Why?"

"Just want to make sure you're relaxed."

"Relaxed? How could I not be? You *relaxed* me all night last night and again this morning. If I were any more relaxed, you'd have to wheel me around on a gurney."

It didn't take long for the doors of the aircraft to close and the captain to announce we were ready for takeoff.

Ghost reached over and intertwined our fingers, giving my hand a squeeze.

"You don't have to worry you know," I told him.

"About what?"

"About me. I know I'm always safe with you. And even if something happens, I know you'll always come to my rescue."

"Goddamn right, I will."

I smiled at the vehemence in his voice, secure in the knowledge Ghost would always be there. Not only for me, but for the baby growing inside me. Our son, or daughter, would always feel his love and protection.

"I love you, Ghost."

"Love you, Princess."

ABOUT THE AUTHOR

Riley Edwards is a bestselling multi-genre author, wife, and military mom. Riley was born and raised in Los Angeles but now resides on the east coast with her fantastic husband and children.

Riley writes heart-stopping romance with sexy alpha heroes and even stronger heroines. Riley's favorite genres to write are romantic suspense and military romance.

Don't forget to sign up for the **Riley's Rebels** mailing list to receive a **FREE COPY of Unbroken** and stay up to date on releases, sales, and giveaways.

Riley Edwards Newsletter –
https://www.subscribepage.com/RRsignup
Add Riley Edwards on Goodreads
http://geni.us/goodreadsre

OTHER BOOKS BY RILEY EDWARDS

AVAILABLE ON AMAZON

The Red Team

Nightstalker

Protecting Olivia

Redeeming Violet

Recovering Ivy

The 707 Freedom Series

Free

Freeing Jasper

Finally Free

Freedom

The Next Generation

All the Pretty Girls

The Gift

The Masters Collection

The Awakening

The Collective

Unbroken 1 & 2 – Season One

Trust – Season Two (Fall of 2018)

There are many more books in this fan fiction world than listed here, for an up-to-date list go to www.AcesPress.com

You can also visit our Amazon page at: http://www.amazon.com/author/operationalpha

Special Forces: Operation Alpha World

Denise Agnew: Dangerous to Hold
Shauna Allen: Awakening Aubrey
Shauna Allen: Defending Danielle
Shauna Allen: Rescuing Rebekah
Shauna Allen: Saving Scarlett
Shauna Allen: Saving Grace
Brynne Asher: Blackburn
Jennifer Becker: Hiding Catherine
Julia Bright: Saving Lorelei
Julia Bright: Rescuing Amy
Victoria Bright: Surviving Savage
Victoria Bright: Going Ghost
Victoria Bright: Jostling Joker
Cara Carnes: Protecting Mari
Kendra Mei Chailyn: Beast
Kendra Mei Chailyn: Barbie
Kendra Mei Chailyn : Pitbull
Melissa Kay Clarke: Rescuing Annabeth
Melissa Kay Clarke: Safeguarding Miley
Samantha A. Cole: Handling Haven

Samantha A. Cole: Cheating the Devil
Sue Coletta: Hacked
Melissa Combs: Gallant
KaLyn Cooper: Rescuing Melina
Liz Crowe: Marking Mariah
Jordan Dane: Redemption for Avery
Jordan Dane: Fiona's Salvation
Riley Edwards: Protecting Olivia
Riley Edwards: Redeeming Violet
Riley Edwards, Recovering Ivy
Nicole Flockton: Protecting Maria
Nicole Flockton: Guarding Erin
Nicole Flockton: Guarding Suzie
Nicole Flockton: Guarding Brielle
Casey Hagen: Shielding Nebraska
Casey Hagen: Shielding Harlow
Casey Hagen: Shielding Josie
Casey Hagen: Shielding Blair
Desiree Holt: Protecting Maddie
Kathy Ivan: Saving Sarah
Kathy Ivan: Saving Savannah
Kathy Ivan: Saving Stephanie
Jesse Jacobson: Protecting Honor
Jesse Jacobson: Fighting for Honor
Jesse Jacobson: Defending Honor
Jesse Jacobson: Summer Breeze
Silver James: Rescue Moon
Silver James: SEAL Moon

Silver James: Assassin's Moon
Silver James: Under the Assassin's Moon
Becca Jameson: Saving Sofia
Kate Kinsley: Protecting Ava
Heather Long: Securing Arizona
Heather Long: Guarding Gertrude
Heather Long: Protecting Pilar
Heather Long: Covering Coco
Gennita Low: No Protection
Kirsten Lynn: Joining Forces for Jesse
Margaret Madigan: Bang for the Buck
Margaret Madigan: Buck the System
Margaret Madigan: Jungle Buck
Margaret Madigan: December Chill
Rachel McNeely: The SEAL's Surprise Baby
Rachel McNeely: The SEAL's Surprise Bride
Rachel McNeely: The SEAL's Surprise Twin
KD Michaels: Saving Laura
KD Michaels: Protecting Shane
KD Michaels: Avenging Angels
Wren Michaels: The Fox & The Hound
Wren Michaels: The Fox & The Hound 2
Wren Michaels: Shadow of Doubt
Wren Michaels: Shift of Fate
Wren Michaels: Steeling His Heart
Kat Mizera: Protecting Bobbi
Mary B Moore: Force Protection
LeTeisha Newton: Protecting Butterfly

LeTeisha Newton: Protecting Goddess
LeTeisha Newton: Protecting Vixen
LeTeisha Newton: Protecting Heartbeat
MJ Nightingale: Protecting Beauty
MJ Nightingale: Betting on Benny
MJ Nightingale: Protecting Secrets
Sarah O'Rourke: Saving Liberty
Debra Parmley: Protecting Pippa
Lainey Reese: Protecting New York
Jenika Snow: Protecting Lily
Jen Talty: Burning Desire
Jen Talty: Burning Kiss
Jen Talty: Burning Skies
Jen Talty: Burning Lies
Jen Talty: Burning Heart
Megan Vernon: Protecting Us
Megan Vernon: Protecting Earth

Fire and Police: Operation Alpha World

KaLyn Cooper: Justice for Gwen
Aspen Drake: Sheltering Emma

As you know, this book included at least one character from Susan Stoker's books. To check out more, see below.

Delta Force Heroes Series

Rescuing Rayne (FREE!)
Rescuing Aimee (novella)
Rescuing Emily
Rescuing Harley
Marrying Emily
Rescuing Kassie
Rescuing Bryn
Rescuing Casey
Rescuing Sadie
Rescuing Wendy
Rescuing Mary (Oct 2018)
Rescuing Macie (April 2019)

Badge of Honor: Texas Heroes Series

Justice for Mackenzie (FREE!)
Justice for Mickie
Justice for Corrie
Justice for Laine (novella)
Shelter for Elizabeth
Justice for Boone
Shelter for Adeline
Shelter for Sophie
Justice for Erin

Justice for Milena
Shelter for Blythe
Justice for Hope (Sept 2018)
Shelter for Quinn (Feb 2019)
Shelter for Koren (June 2019)
Shelter for Penelope (Oct 2019)

SEAL of Protection Series

Protecting Caroline (FREE!)
Protecting Alabama
Protecting Fiona
Marrying Caroline (novella)
Protecting Summer
Protecting Cheyenne
Protecting Jessyka
Protecting Julie (novella)
Protecting Melody
Protecting the Future
Protecting Kiera (novella)
Protecting Dakota

SEAL of Protection: Legacy Series

Securing Caite (Jan 2019)
Securing Sidney (May 2019)
Securing Piper (Sept 2019)
Securing Zoey (TBA)
Securing Avery (TBA)
Securing Kalee (TBA)

New York Times, *USA Today* and *Wall Street Journal* Bestselling Author Susan Stoker has a heart as big as the state of Texas where she lives, but this all American girl has also spent the last fourteen years living in Missouri, California, Colorado, and Indiana. She's married to a retired Army man who now gets to follow *her* around the country.

She debuted her first series in 2014 and quickly followed that up with the SEAL of Protection Series, which solidified her love of writing and creating stories readers can get lost in.

If you enjoyed this book, or any book, please consider leaving a review. It's appreciated by authors more than you'll know.

www.stokeraces.com

www.AcesPress.com

susan@stokeraces.com

Made in the USA
Columbia, SC
11 June 2024